OLIVER TWIST INVESTIGATES

Who killed Nancy? Did Charles Dickens frame Bill Sikes? And if so, why? As an adult, Oliver Twist receives deeply unsettling information. Written years earlier by Fagin, as he awaited execution, it convinces Oliver that Dickens was not entirely truthful about Nancy's death. Oliver, compelled to investigate, is drawn into the slums of London, to seek out some of the figures from his past — Betsy, Noah Claypole, Mr Bumble, Charley Bates and — the Artful Dodger. Oliver's life is set to change dramatically as he uncovers not only what happened to Nancy, but also the astonishing truth about his own identity . . .

04599677

Brought up in the north-east, G.M. Best studied history at Exeter College, Oxford and went on to become the headmaster of Kingswood School in Bath. He has written widely on Methodist history and has also penned a musical called *Marley's Ghosts*, based on the work of Gilbert and Sullivan. He is currently Warden of the New Room in Bristol, a research fellow at Wesley College, Bristol, and a member of the Methodist Heritage Committee.

G. M. BEST

OLIVER TWIST INVESTIGATES

Complete and Unabridged

ULVERSCROFT
Leicester

First published in Great Britain in 2010 by
Robert Hale Limited
London

First Large Print Edition
published 2012
by arrangement with
Robert Hale Limited
London

Copyright © 2010 by G. M. Best

British Library CIP Data

Best, G. M.
  Oliver Twist investigates.
  1. Murder- -Investigation- -England- -London- -History- -
  19th century- -Fiction. 2. London (England)- -Social
  conditions- -19th century- -Fiction. 3. Dickens, Charles,
  1812 – 1870- -Fiction. 4. Detective and mystery stories.
  5. Large type books.
  I. Title
  823.9'2–dc23

  ISBN 978–1–4448–0955–8

Published by
F. A. Thorpe (Publishing)
Anstey, Leicestershire

Set by Words & Graphics Ltd.
Anstey, Leicestershire
Printed and bound in Great Britain by
T. J. International Ltd., Padstow, Cornwall

This book is printed on acid-free paper

Contents

Preface

The manuscript from which this book is drawn was discovered entirely by accident buried amid a trunkful of other Victorian documents which were purchased at auction on the off-chance that they might contain something of interest. I have no way of verifying its authenticity or that of the attached letter, which I have incorporated and which purports to have been written by Fagin. All I have done is to amend some of the faulty spelling and punctuation and create headings for the chapters into which I have chosen to divide the manuscript. I cannot account for how the manuscript ended up within the trunk I purchased, or why the documents were not originally published (other than that there is a reference within the manuscript itself to delaying publication until no participant could be damaged by what the manuscript reveals). I therefore leave it to the reader to judge whether this is just a clever Victorian forgery or whether Oliver Twist was not just a fictional character invented by Charles Dickens but, rather, a real boy, who, in his adult life, wrote this true account of who really murdered the prostitute Nancy and why.

For my part I think the manuscript is true. Charles Dickens was renowned for using his personal life and experiences within his novels and it seems to me not unreasonable to believe that *Oliver Twist*, written when he was still essentially a journalist rather than a famous novelist, was perhaps more personal than anyone has previously supposed. The manuscript certainly gives interesting and plausible reasons for some of Dickens' unusual personal behaviour and even hints at where his inspiration came from for another of his great novels, *Great Expectations*. True or false, this book certainly delivers a totally new twist on the tale of the boy who dared to ask for more by providing more from the boy himself.

G.M. Best (editor)

1

Truth Will Out

Nightmares about Nancy dominated my troubled childhood years. I could not shake from my mind an image of her battered and bruised body in that blood-spattered room of betrayal. But that is not surprising. As a child I had been repeatedly told how she had faced such a vicious beating that it had rendered her fair face virtually featureless. You may recall that, in describing the events of her brutal murder, Charles Dickens wrote how the following morning the bright sunlight caused a reflection from the horrifying pool of gore to quiver and dance on the ceiling of the room and so frightenly emphasize her utter destruction. It was not just Bill Sikes who found this intolerable. So did I in my imagination. And the passage of time did nothing to silence the sound of her frantic screams reverberating ever louder within my mind, pleading for assistance which neither I nor anyone else could provide. I could not forget that this nightmare scene of utter brutality stemmed entirely from her efforts to protect me from Fagin and Sikes. Her dull and lifeless eyes reproached me for the destruction I had brought upon her. Awake or asleep, I struggled under their gaze, knowing I was totally unworthy of her sacrifice and suffering.

Put bluntly, I never felt my miserable life was one worth saving. If you have read the great novelist's version of my early years, you will know I was born an unwanted bastard and named Oliver Twist thanks to the whim of the resentful local authorities, into whose reluctant hands I was placed following the death of my mother in childbirth. I survived the manifold minor cruelties of the parish workhouse only to be sold like a slave because, driven by sheer starvation, I had the temerity to dare to ask for more gruel to eat. The good men of the parish judged me to be an ungrateful wretch destined for the hangman's rope and Mr Bumble, the fat and choleric parochial beadle, handed me over for my impious and profane offence to one of his friends. This was the local undertaker, a gaunt, large-jointed man called Sowerberry, who paid the princely sum of five pounds for me. For a few months I acted as a deaf mute, walking in silent procession in front of the corpses of children and wishing I could change places with them. Sowerberry believed my sickly, white, tormented face, which bore all the signs of years of suffering, ideal for this purpose.

I believe Mr Sowerberry, despite his trade in death, was kindly disposed towards me but his foul-tempered wife took an instant dislike to me and made my life a living hell. As far as she was concerned, any workhouse brat was not worth keeping. She only fed me on the foul scraps judged unsuitable for their dog and she made me sleep in a coffin for my bed. The nightly horror of sleeping amid the stench of the dead was only matched by the brutal treatment that I received at the hands of Sowerbery's simpering daughter, Charlotte, and her lascivious lover, Noah Claypole. They delighted in tormenting me, knowing I was friendless and unprotected. Noah called me 'a regular right-down bad 'un' and so I believed myself to be. When I eventually responded to my cruel persecution by assaulting him, I was locked up and beaten by Bumble, who, bully that he was, took a perverse delight in savagely punishing me.

Although I was just a child, I was filled with sufficient fear and loathing to flee my persecutors. I managed to escape from the undertaker's house and walked about seventy-five miles over the next seven days, determined to reach London and escape any pursuit. My shoeless feet became blistered and bloody, and my legs trembled beneath me for lack of food. All I had to eat was the occasional crust of bread and draught of water donated at the cottage doors at which I begged. I slept where I could in wet hedges and roadside ditches and not all those I met were kind to a vagrant, even if he was but a pitifully weak child of nine years old. There were too many roaming beggars prepared to steal from the unsuspecting for me to be welcomed. Some set their vicious dogs on me and others offered me only a hellish curse or the threat of prison. Exhausted and malnourished by the time I got as far as Barnet, it is not surprising that I fell easy victim to the charms of a common-faced boy pickpocket called Jack Dawkins, who appeared to offer me genuine friendly assistance by agreeing to take me to his lodgings in the great city.

Though only a few years older than I, Jack had all the airs and manners of a man. Indeed he wore a man's coat, even though it reached nearly to his heels. He was, as Dickens later described him, an 'Artful Dodger', a roistering and swaggering a young gentleman as ever stood four feet six, or something less. Unfortunately, he did not have 'thief' branded on his forehead or 'pickpocket' inscribed on his clothes, and so, born trickster that he was, he had only to exert a tiny fraction of his natural charm to entrap me. I didn't realize that he was befriending me in order that I could become a member of the same thieving gang for whom he worked and which was run by a fence named Fagin, a man who was to treat me worse than all those who had gone before.

My senses were overwhelmed with my first taste of London — its buildings garbed with soot, its thoroughfares jam-packed with a jostling humanity, and its streets filled with rotting and stinking debris. The sheer volume and variety of sounds that pounded my brain were terrifying as iron-clad wheels rattled over cobbled streets and an endless succession of hawkers and sellers yelled out their wares. No conversation was possible unless we shouted to each other. All around us were people who seemed to care only for themselves — slipping and sliding, pushing and bumping, cursing and swearing. Worst of all, my lungs were filled for the first time with that horrific stench which stems not only from hundreds of thousands of unwashed people but also from the city's countless smoking and reeking chimneys, its dung-pits and sewage-filled alleyways, and its endless succession of breweries, tanneries, foundries and other industrial buildings.

At first we passed through busy broad streets lined with pleasantly proportioned buildings and attractive shops, but soon we entered narrow and overcrowded alleys where drunken men and women wallowed in filth and where every conceivable crime was in evidence. When we reached our destination, it was a disgustingly dirty building off a tiny courtyard that was filled with the charnel stench of a nearby overfilled graveyard. The Dodger gave a whistle to signal our presence and we were soon admitted. At one time it must have been a grand place because the rooms upstairs had great high wooden chimneypieces and large doors, with panelled walls and cornices to the ceilings. However, everything was now worm-eaten and black with neglect and dust. All the mouldering shutters were fast closed and the bars that held them were screwed tight into the wood, so the only light admitted was that which stole its way through round holes at the top. Generations of spiders had built their webs in the angles of its walls and ceilings and, as we walked, I could hear the sound of rats or mice scampering back to their holes over the straw-filled billets and mounds of filthy rags which seemed to account for the house's main furniture.

When we entered the main room of the

house it was lit by a candle stuck in a ginger-beer bottle. I found myself in the midst of a crowd of boys of varying ages with nothing natural to youth about them. Though they appeared at first to be friendly, I soon found that they were low-browed, vicious, cunning, wicked creatures, utterly ignorant and speeding down to their own destruction. Throughout my life I had been ill used, but it did not prepare me for the hellhole that was Fagin's lair or for the cruelties I would experience at the hands of their master, the old Jew himself. At night I had to struggle with the other boys to find body space on the filthy floor and I shall never eradicate from my mind Fagin's repulsive and villainous face, his dirty, matted hair, and his shrivelled, grasping hands.

Believe me when I say that Charles Dickens's account was a sanitized version of what happened next. Fagin soon had me trained to join his team of pickpockets and his fiendish depravity made my life even more worthless. No one, let alone Nancy, should have died to save my sin-ridden skin. And such a sacrifice was unnecessary. Those of you who have read Dickens's account of my life will know that for a brief time I was rescued from a potential life of crime by the blessed benevolence of a gentleman named

Mr Brownlow. This kind soul saw that I was an unwilling thief on my first attempt at picking the pockets of his bottle-green coat as he browsed at a bookstall. When he rescued me from the stiff-necked magistrate who would have consigned me to prison, it was the first act of genuine goodness I had ever experienced. It still brings tears to my eyes when I recall my wonderment at this gold-spectacled benefactor, who was prepared to take a wretch like me into his home and offer such lavish care and attention. And I was doubly blessed because his house-keeper, Mrs Bedwin, was equally kind to me, lovely woman that she was. Only her generous heart matched her ample girth. In many respects she became the mother I had never had.

My brief period of happiness in Mr Brownlow's home ended when Fagin ensured my recapture by using the prostitute Nancy to pose as my sister. She thought Fagin's motive in regaining control of me was his fear of what I might say about his activities to the police, but he had other reasons. Unbeknown to her, I had a half-brother called Edward Leeford, who had claimed an inheritance that should have been mine and who, under the assumed name of Monks, had instigated an investigation into my whereabouts. Fagin had met Monks and been handsomely paid to ensure that I rejoined his gang. Monks wanted me to become a thief and so end my life on the gallows. Nancy dressed for the occasion and, always the consummate actress, seized me in the street whilst I was on an errand returning some books for Mr Brownlow. Nancy claimed that I had run away from home and that I needed rescuing from my criminal associates. She played her part so well that not one passer-by heeded my protests or cries for help. I was thus easily reconsigned to Hell.

Yet it was also this same Nancy who then became my champion, preventing Fagin inflicting some of his worst excesses on me and bearing the blows of her lover, Bill Sikes, rather than permit him to beat me. I can hear her voice now, courageously telling them she could not bear to see me become a thing of the streets like her. Is it any wonder that I soon forgave her for her role in my capture and came to adore her? Who could not love Nancy? She was the one blossom in our dung heap, the one constant source of light in our darkness. If I were asked to define the word 'beautiful' I would simply utter her name. She was strikingly attractive in shape and character. Her vivacious smile, her sparkling eyes, and her infectious good humour made her unforgettable. Though she had little cause to celebrate and much to be sorrowful about, she was so full of fun that she lightened the darkest mood of those around her. The day's events appeared brighter to all Fagin's gang when viewed through her eyes, and, amid the brutal nature of much of our existence, it was her innumerable little acts of kindness that made our broken lives bearable. In a society where few trusted anyone, all trusted her and I hung on her every word and gesture.

Don't mistake my meaning. Nancy was no angel. Her language could be unbelievably coarse, her humour vulgar and lewd. When crossed, her temper was sometimes foul if usually short-lived. However, these few failings never detracted from her ability to rise above the harshness that surrounded us. She was especially adept at poking fun at the pompous and the proud, and her uncanny ability to mimic the characteristics of the people she had met during the course of the day was unfailingly comical. Above everything else, Nancy was loyal to her friends, even when, like me, they least deserved it. Afterwards I assumed she especially sought to protect me because she was outraged at overhearing the plans of Monks and Fagin to destroy me. She rescued me from what he and Fagin intended by betraying vital information to Mr Brownlow who, as it later became clear, had been the closest friend of my and Monks's father.

Thus it came about that, when Sikes forced me to assist in a burglary, I was rescued and given refuge in the very home he and Fagin had wanted me to rob. There I first met Rose Maylie, whom Monks later revealed to be my aunt. Rose was a very different character from Nancy. She was gentler and sweeter and infinitely more innocent, but she shared Nancy's passion for justice. Many a fine lady would have despised and scorned any contact with a prostitute, but Rose's innate courage enabled her to override the dictates of propriety and her natural sensitivity enabled her to discern Nancy's qualities. I have been blessed to know two such strong-minded if widely different women. Curiously, it was Nancy rather than Rose who found their meetings difficult. I think that when she saw Rose, Nancy was reminded of how different her own life might have been and that frightened her. Corrupted as her life had become, she feared that she could not live the reformed life that Rose offered her. Her uncharacteristic lack of confidence and her undoubted, if misplaced, love for the villainous Bill Sikes made Nancy refuse to accept Mr Brownlow's proffered protection following my rescue.

My last contact with Nancy was the farewell kiss she gave me before she returned to Fagin's gang. It was the last time any of us saw her alive. The discovery of her battered and bludgeoned body seemed to point to only one conclusion. Her lover, Bill Sikes, who had led the abortive burglary attempt, had murdered her for her treachery, egged on by a furious Fagin. As news of the brutal manner of her death became widely known, I recognized that everyone bar Mr Brownlow and Rose Maylie cared far more about Nancy's death than they did about my escape from Fagin's embrace. The subsequent accident in which Sikes hanged himself whilst trying to escape capture did not change that, nor did Fagin's imprisonment and subsequent condemnation and execution. If it had not been for me, Nancy would have lived. I had deprived the dregs of society of one of their few joys.

For a number of years after Nancy's martyrdom I dared aspire to justify the expenditure of her blood by helping those unfortunate children who live — if it can be called living — amid the same kind of depravity and destitution from which she rescued me. I encouraged Mr Brownlow, who became my guardian, to use the little wealth he had to offer refuge to those who had experienced little love in their lives and for whom neglect, cruelty and crushing poverty were the norm of their existence. If my efforts made a difference to a few, I am glad, but such satisfaction as it gave did not ease my conscience or salve my sense of guilt. In my mind neither my good deeds nor my improved station in society made up one jot for the crushing of Nancy's skull and the silencing of her laughter.

Some might think that I would rejoice in having my history recorded by so remarkable a writer as Charles Dickens, but I can assure you the opposite was true. It did not help me that Dickens had etched Nancy's murder into the very fabric of British society. Through the skill of his pen the whole world felt that Nancy's death was the worst of all the bad deeds committed in London under cover of darkness. His powerful depiction of her destruction at the hands of her lover, Bill Sikes, convinced a generation that it was the foulest and cruellest of all the horrors that ever rose with an ill scent upon the morning's miasmic air. Sideshows and theatres put on their own versions of my story, competing to depict as gruesomely as possible Nancy's slaughter for having the temerity to protect me from the machinations of Fagin and

Monks. As I walked the streets their posters constantly reminded me that I would always be seen as the pauper saved by a prostitute. I resented the fact that Dickens was able to move on from the story of Oliver Twist to fresh writing triumphs whilst leaving me trapped in his literary past. Believe me, it is not easy to be always viewed as the emaciated and maltreated workhouse boy who asked for more.

My search for what really happened to Nancy began a few days after my twenty-first birthday in December 1846 when I was summoned to meet a solicitor by the name of Barnabus Moulton, ostensibly in order to hear news of 'a former friend'. I must confess it was my curiosity rather than any hope of renewing contact with a previous acquaintance that drew me to respond. I was unaware that I had any friends from my past! Moulton's chambers were in a decaying and rather forbidding-looking house in Cook's Court. The day was already closing in and the gaslights were newly lit but not yet effective when I arrived. A servant ushered me into a gloomy, cavernous, and ill-decorated room, which smelt heavily of books and leather. In its centre was a large oaken table surrounded by heavy, broad-backed old-fashioned mahogany chairs, whose seats were so covered with documents and files as to make impossible any chance of their serving their original purpose. Old books and ancient parchments, yellowed with age, were thrown in no apparent order across the top of the table, making it also unusable save for the collection of dust. Bookcases, filled with countless volumes, covered all the walls bar one. On its grimy surface hung a large oil painting of a man whose stern demeanour seemed to judge all who entered. Beneath it, with his back towards me, sat a grey-haired figure dressed entirely in black, working at a small desk on which stood two silver antique candlesticks. They gave off insufficient light to the room as a whole but enough to enable him to continue his studies.

When Moulton turned I saw his likeness to the portrait, which was either of him or his father. He rose and, despite a twist of the gout, rapidly advanced towards me, holding out his gnarled hand in greeting. He was older than I had expected and would clearly never see seventy again, but there was no frailty about his rather dour manner. His deep-socketed eyes were cool and direct rather than welcoming and his handshake was firm and dry. He effortlessly set me at my ease. His every gesture seemed to epitomize patience and probity. Had I known whom he represented I would have been less sure of his

15

trustworthiness, but I was naïvely innocent of any suspicion. It therefore came as a great shock when he informed me that he was working on behalf of Fagin. My horror at hearing this name prevented me from departing immediately. I was rooted to the spot as I recalled so vividly the man who had scarred my childhood in ways Dickens had not permitted his pen to portray because of the hypocritical sensitivities of our society. Images of our association flashed through my mind and made me feel physically sick.

Yet Moulton appeared oblivious of my state. He told me in a matter-of-fact tone how Fagin, shortly before he was to be publicly hanged for his crimes, had written what he chose to call 'a final testament'. He had given strict instructions that it should be kept in a vault until I was fully a man. After I had come of age, Moulton had been told to hand over the document to me. Saying this, he unlocked a small drawer in the desk, pulled out a slim, dusty envelope, and handed it towards me. I made no move to accept the proffered package but he insisted, telling me I could always destroy it unopened and unread if I so desired. He literally pressed the loathsome object into my trembling hands, and I was in so much inward turmoil I did not resist. I cannot even recall how I left his chambers but

I somehow pulled myself together and did, thrusting Fagin's testament into one of my pockets.

Once back in my room, only the lack of a fire prevented me from burning the envelope's contents unopened. I suspect if Mr Brownlow had still been alive I would have sought some other means of destruction, because that is undoubtedly what he would have advised me to do. However, to my intense grief, my dearest guardian and friend had died the previous year, bequeathing to me all that remained of his fortune, which turned out to be quite a respectable amount and far more than I had expected — enough to make me a reasonably wealthy man. I felt I had no other person in whom I could confide, other than Mrs Bedwin, Mr Brownlow's former housekeeper, but I was reluctant to involve her in my sordid past. In the end my curiosity overcame my circumspection and, with shaking hands, I took a thin knife and slit open what Moulton had given me. Inside the envelope were some dirty sheets of paper. These were covered with a scrawling handwriting, which, even after the passage of so many years, I easily identified as Fagin's script. After a momentary hesitation I reluctantly began to read his testament and what he revealed then consigned all my certainties to oblivion. Thus was he able to strike at me from beyond the grave. I could not have been more mistaken when I thought the Jew's influence on my life had ended on my final visit to his prison cell.

On that morning Fagin, condemned to the gallows and filth-encrusted with the stinking debris of his prison cell, looked more like a snared beast than a man. No longer buoyed up by some vague and undefined hope of reprieve or some even wilder idea of escape, his once sharp mind had become semi-deranged by fear and an overwhelming sense of his helplessness. He had exhausted his attendants with importunities and now he alternated between demanding what right anyone had to butcher him and whimpering childishly for my forgiveness. Despite my obvious reluctance to go anywhere near him, he had tried to clutch me to his chest, seeming to think that in some magical way I could ensure his escape. Not that I would have helped him had it been within my power. I knew too much of his crimes to wish his release from the noose. The words of forgiveness that he extracted from me gave him false hope because they contained no element of truth. They were just said in fear. When I left rejoicing from his cell the howling cries of his anguish, which reverberated around the prison, rang in my ears for days but they caused me no loss of sleep at night.

It is therefore the paradox to end all paradoxes that I should have discovered Dickens's story of my early life to be false through this foul man, whose whole life was a constant lie and to whom the truth was always an anathema. For reasons that will become obvious, his account launched me on to the investigative journey that these pages record. What follows is my attempt to set the record straight. Dickens's account of my early life turned out to be just a beautifully written lie by a reporter extraordinaire, who put his fiction before fact. What you are about to read is the truth although I know it lacks the literary skill of the master writer who first penned my tale. Through its pages I will reveal to you the real reason why Nancy loved me more than anyone else in the world. I will tell you the truth of what happened after Sikes had been consumed by rage at Fagin's account of Nancy's treacherous actions. Oh yes, her precious blood did stain the carpet red, seeping into the paws of Bill's dog and thus marking her alleged murderer's final journeying. But I assure you, Sikes struck no fatal blow. Nancy was not bludgeoned to death by his savage blows.

I was rescued from my nightmares when I

discovered they had no basis in reality, but increasingly now I feel that Nancy's spirit cries out for Bill Sikes's name to be rescued from the ignominy into which it has fallen. It was entirely another hand that caused Nancy to breathe her last. I have ensured that my account of what really happened to Nancy will lie undiscovered and unread for many years simply because my revelations have the power to hurt the living, not least me. However, there will come a time when this is no longer so, and I hope a future generation will then cease to revel in Dickens's story and people will at last understand the real tragedy that surrounded Nancy. Writing what follows has evoked very painful memories and yet it has never made me regret opening Fagin's letter. Foul and crude though its contents are, they set me on to the path that led to the truth. Maybe therefore his testament is his damned soul's one claim to mercy. If so, let God forgive him his many misdeeds because I cannot. Read it and I think you will see why.

2

Fagin's Final Testament

My dear boy, I know you will be surprised to hear from me after all these intervening years, but I have every confidence that my presence will still be very much with you. I was always master to those I met and you were always very special to me. You don't need me to remind you of that, do you?

I awoke, cold and wretched, on this, my final morning. Only the thought of our meeting and what I had to tell you sustained me. When I saw that that interfering prude, Brownlow, was accompanying you, it was the cruellest blow because I knew then that we could not be alone together. I found our final meeting such a painful one, not least because I could not voice what I really intended to say. This letter will tell you that which I was unable to say to you then. I have deliberately arranged that this letter should not be sent to you until your entry into full manhood. If it were to be delivered straight away, I am pretty sure that meddlesome fool Brownlow would never let you see its contents. This testament will serve a double purpose. I write to undeceive you about the events of your youth and, in so doing, perhaps make some amends. But this document also lets you know, Oliver, the extent to which I am still thinking of you, the loveliest of all my boys.

As I pen this I can hear the sound of St Sepulchre's and of the gallows being prepared for me and the memory of past pleasures is all I have left before I face that hideous apparatus of death. My dear boy let me indulge in a little reminiscing. Our first meeting is engraved on my memory. I hope it is equally so on yours. It was after the Artful Dodger found you wandering the streets, fresh from your flight from old Sowerberry and your ill treatment as an undertaker's mute. Jack's talents did not just lie in theft. He always had a soft spot for a pretty face. He brought you into my home whilst I was cooking some sausages for my sweet little boys. I recall you were such an innocent child and you stared at all the silk pocket-handkerchiefs that hung in the room with no notion as to why they were all there. I told you they were all ready for the wash, much to the amusement of the lads. Your gullibility, while it lasted, was a delight we all enjoyed.

Though you were at first naïvely innocent, it soon became obvious to me that you were also intelligent. I like that in a boy. A beautiful body without a mind is only half the pleasure. Though exhausted from your travels, you were very quick to espy my hidden wealth that very day. When we had all fed and the lads had gone out to do some more work, I thought you were asleep because of the gin I had given you and so, deceived, I inspected my rings, brooches, bracelets, and other jewellery, with their costly workmanship and magnificent materials. You had a unique ability to be always in the wrong place at the wrong time. But you didn't deceive me for long, did you, my dear? Remember how I placed the bread knife at your sweet delicate throat and asked you to forget you had seen my precious treasures, all that I hoped to live on in my old age? Remember your punishment, Oliver? How I asked you to wash before me? That revealed other treasures, didn't it? You were such a beautiful boy. And beautiful things are there to be enjoyed, aren't they, my dear?

Do you still recall the rest of that first full day with us? I remember it as if it was yesterday. I was greatly amused that Jack Dawkins and Charley Bates found you such a prig. I played the merry gentleman and placed a snuffbox in one pocket, a notecase in another, and a watch in a third. Then I placed a chain round my neck and a diamond pin in my shirt, and pretended to be out shopping. Jack and Charley showed all their superb skills to rob me of the items without my noticing. And you were so delightfully green and naïve. You never saw the fondling that accompanied the filching. They weren't just groping for handkerchiefs and wallets that day, Oliver, as you later came to appreciate. Stealing has such a wonderful feel to it if it's done properly. And I always gave my personal attention to all my protégés, ensuring you were all taught exactly what was expected.

And then Nancy and Bet joined us. You thought they were such nice girls, although we could still smell the semen on them from their latest clients. But then you didn't yet know that pleasure, did you, Oliver? As you read this you will have come of age and probably experienced the favours of prostitutes. If so, you'll know the delights of women don't match up to the little games we used to play. Just you, me, Charley and Jack. A sweet little foursome fondling and searching each other's treasures. It pained me greatly that your oft-expressed desire to go on to the streets with the lads was not the product of a wish to widen your experience but to escape it. I don't mind admitting, my dear boy, I didn't want to part company with you. I had no problem taking payment from Monks to arrange for your career with us to become a permanent one. I was being paid for what was supremely pleasurable.

Although our acquaintance had just begun, I missed your pallid beauty desperately when the damned police took you because they believed you had stolen things from old Brownlow. Hence my determination to get you back, especially when I heard you were in a bed in his house. My bed was where I wanted you to be. So I had Nancy pretend to be your sister so she could reclaim you. That was how you first met Bill and his ferocious dog, Bull's-eye. Which did you fear most, Oliver? The cur or the curses? The fierce growling of that savage creature or the blows of Bill? And Mr Brownlow had given you such fine clothes to wear. Remember how Charley and Jack admired them and gradually began to strip you of them? You knew then how keen we were to see you again. And all you could do was ungratefully plead for mercy and beg to be sent back to that old man. Did he treat you better than us? Were his embraces more to your taste?

It wasn't the way to greet old friends. You can't blame us for encouraging Bull's-eye to attack you. Love-bites were all we wanted and you were playing so hard to get. When Nancy intervened so aggressively to protect you, I failed to recognize it as a warning sign that she might become a danger to all of us. It was seeing you stripped to the waist. It betrayed to her your origin because the scars on your shoulders marked you as a workhouse brat. It's beyond me why someone should savagely beat a boy when there is so much pleasure to be had in other ways, but few escape permanent damage that pass through its care. You certainly hadn't. And suddenly there is Nancy, herself born and bred in its uncharitable environs, threatening to put that old fool Bumble's mark on all of us rather than see you hurt further. Her face white with rage, her emotion so high she bit her lower lip till the blood flowed. She swore she would rather have died than bring you back to us.

Bill had to shake her more than a little, didn't he, my dear, shake her till she fainted away. You later saw the livid bruises on her arms and neck. They were the first signs of the brutality she was to bear for your sake. And much of it in vain as was certainly the case this time. With her lying unconscious, Charley showed you the way to bed again and undressed you fully. I'm sure he lived up to his name of Master Bates. He had such a unique talent in that direction. Always a pleasure to watch him at work, although you were not — how shall I put it? — very forthcoming at the time. I seem to remember we had to resort to solitary confinement to win more co-operation from you. And we talked of the many delights of hanging — rather ironic in view of my position now. They say that a man gets an erection when he's hung. Well, Oliver, you'll still be in my thoughts as the very noose tightens around my neck and it will not be the rope that brings me a final pleasure. My dear boy, does the image of my love give you secret delight? As a man, can you bear to caress another and not think of my caresses? No amount of contrition can erase our past. Think of it, Oliver, just you and I damned together for eternity for our actions.

But the memory of past pleasures leads me to digress. As I have intimated, Nancy's view of you changed when she saw your workhouse origins. I later discovered it was not the scars that had moved her so greatly but a small birthmark visible on your back. It made her desperate to discover more about you. This was an easy task for her to accomplish. You had told most of your story to the Dodger and he was always ready to spend the time of day with Nancy. It turned out that the workhouse from which you had escaped was the same one into which I had forced Nancy to surrender her own bastard child some years ago. A bastard child with a birthmark very similar to the one you carry. Brownlow may have imagined he saw a family resemblance in your features and Monks may have believed you to be his half-brother, but Nancy saw in you her own long-lost child. That is why she was prepared to do anything to save you and why it was only on the night she was murdered that you really became an orphan. So you see, my dear boy, your ancestry truly fitted you to be one of us.

Nancy was able to enlist the help of the up and coming journalist Dickens, whom she had met in earlier days. I shouldn't be surprised if it was more than words between them. He's a handsome, high-spirited, energetic chap, even if his clothes are a bit loud for a gentleman and his speech a trifle too affected. I have good reason to detest the man but I can see why ladies would like him, with his fresh-faced pinky complexion, fine forehead, firmly set mouth, and expressive eyes. And Nancy had a way with the toffs. It was probably part payment for pleasing him so much that made Dickens express his willingness to help her rescue you from me. And together they came up with a plan. Nancy would pretend to go along with my desire to ensure you became a full-blown thief. She would ensure that we got wind of a house ripe for the plucking. In reality the inmates of that house, who were known to Dickens, would be tipped off about the burglary. They would be waiting for the break-in and they would ensure you were retaken from us. It almost all went like clockwork. Bill and his mate, Toby Crackit, took you on their ill-fated expedition, much to your terror at the time. They found the house, broke through one of its small windows, and thrust you inside so you could then let them in by the street door. Your rescuers were at hand and fired their guns to serve a double purpose. They wanted not only to send Bill and Toby running, but also to make them believe you had been wounded and probably killed. Nancy had the sense to appreciate your future would only become secure if Monks and I believed you were dead.

I was horrified by the news, not least because for a time I did indeed believe you had been killed. However, I sent out my spies and it wasn't long before your survival was known. And, indeed, your story then acquired a wider fame because Dickens betrayed both you and Nancy. He saw in your tribulations a perfect story to help him achieve fame by uncovering the horrors of the workhouse system. He began writing in monthly installments about you, although he must have known it would endanger Nancy's life and your future. People say he is a great writer and that he has a strong social concern to help others. I think he had a stronger desire to become famous. You and poor Nancy were just steps to that.

Contrast Dickens's motives with mine and then you'll see you meant more to me than to him. I, who hate travelling, even journeyed with that sniveller Monks when he proved determined to see you. I wanted to ensure he brought no harm to you. We had to tread carefully to avoid detection by those who guarded you, but we did manage one evening to draw near to the house unseen. My heart leapt when I saw you sitting asleep by the window, still clutching in your hands the book you had been reading. The jessamine and honeysuckle that crept over the casement were not as attractive to my nostrils as the smell of your sweet, sweet body. Who knows what Monks would have done had he been alone. He was so consumed with rage at the sight of you, it was all I could do to restrain him from climbing through the window. As it was, it was my efforts to draw him away which aroused you from your slumber. You screamed for help when you saw me, but there was no need, Oliver. I was only protecting you from Monks.

But let me come to the point. It was your precious Dickens who informed me of Nancy's treachery. He wasn't the first and he won't be the last journalist to betray his sources. He even sent me advance information of her intended meeting with Brownlow and Rose Maylie, counting on me to ensure she was removed. Believe me, Dickens wanted Nancy killed. And the more brutal the method the better. And I, blind fool that I was, did what he expected. All I could think about was that Nancy had ensured you might never again be in my hands. She had no right to do that and her actions endangered us all. You knew too much about us all for your escape to be ignored.

Beside myself with a mixture of jealousy and fear, I told Bill what Dickens had told me. I spelt out to him how she had given him laudanum to send him to sleep so that she could steal out at night to find those most interested in our downfall and peach to them. I got young Bolter to tell how he'd followed her and seen her meet a gentleman and a lady. He spelt out how she had told against us without her being under any kind of threat or compulsion. I will not pretend ignorance. I knew what reaction all this would evoke in

Bill. Even at the best of times, he was an easy man to arouse. He left me with such anger and bitterness in his heart that I knew what the outcome would be and I rejoiced at the prospect of what he would do to her. I felt certain he would dance to my tune.

But, remember, Oliver, Dickens used me as much as I used Bill. Can you imagine what it's like for me to know I was tricked into actions that have condemned me to the gallows and not to know the reason why Dickens did what he did? If so, you'll know why I want you now to find out why he wanted Nancy dead. I want you to seek out the truth so that old Fagin will have the last laugh over this alleged great writer. His motive must be one he wants hidden from the world and I want you to expose it. It's in your interests to do so because, believe me, Dickens knows more about Nancy and about your birth than he has written about, and you know less about your origins than you think. You see, dear boy, I cannot comment on Nancy's belief that you might be her child but I can say I think you are not and never were any relation to the Maylies or to Monks. It is my view that Nancy will have revealed to Dickens secrets about your birth. Secrets that she kept hidden from me and from Bill and from you. Those secrets may have cost Nancy her life. Certainly they were secrets that Dickens hoped would die with her.

I have to stop now. I gather the preparations for my public farewell are complete and so my time on this unpleasant earth is about to end. I will soon have the white cap placed over my face and the noose looped around my neck. I doubt whether anyone will grieve over my departure and, whilst frightened of the fate that awaits me, I am not sorry to leave this bleak stone dungeon and even bleaker world. I have screamed and shouted enough in this place. However, I will die happier if you find out the truth about Charles Dickens's relationship with Nancy, if not for my sake, then for yours. And if not for your sake, then for hers. Find out why Nancy had to die. What secret did she possess that made him want to ensure her destruction?

And so, my dear boy, I wish you the fondest of farewells, knowing for certain you will always have cause to remember me till you join me in death,

With all my fondest love,
Fagin.

3

A Hint of Blackmail

Fagin's letter swept away all my pretence of
having acquired respectability. I found that
his death had not erased one jot of the power
he still held over me. The memories I had
desperately sought to suppress about the
abuse I had faced at his hands now resurfaced
with an intensity that was almost overpower-
ing. A noose round the neck was insufficient
punishment for one who had totally destroyed
not only my childhood but also that of many
others. Such were my emotions that I came
out in a cold sweat and I physically trembled.
Indeed my stomach churned to such an
extent that I was thrice violently sick. Having
been brought up in a workhouse, I was no
innocent child, but even its dehumanizing
horrors had not prepared me for what I had
faced in the sinful clutches of that most evil
of men. And what made the memory worse
was that, though my brain told me that I was
the victim — just like all those before me who
had taken his fancy — I still felt that
somehow I too was to blame for what

happened. Had I somehow encouraged his attentions? I had been a mere child, lost and friendless, yet still could I not have resisted more? Should I not have embraced death in preference to Fagin's hideous embraces?

What made matters worse was that his letter insidiously poisoned all the very things that had helped me survive. The birthmark I could not dispute, for I had known of its existence for as long as I could remember, but did it truly mark me as Nancy's bastard child? Was I really born to be a member of Fagin's gang? Had Nancy actually tricked Bill Sikes into securing my release by arranging that ill-fated burglary? And how on earth had she secured the assistance of Charles Dickens? Surely Fagin was wrong in insinuating that it was payment for her favours? A man like him would scarce stoop so low as to seek pleasure from such a low-born prostitute, however charming she could be. And what of Fagin's story of betrayal? Had Dickens truly engineered Nancy's murder by betraying her to Fagin in the knowledge that this would evoke Bill Sikes's ruthless anger? It seemed to me to be nonsense but, at the same time, I could not see why Fagin should be challenging me to find out why Dickens had wanted Nancy murdered unless there was some truth in his tale.

My inner turmoil was not helped by the fact Fagin had brought into question my relationship with Agnes Fleming and therefore with her sister, Rose Maylie, the person I had come to look upon as my aunt and whom I most loved in the world now that Mr Brownlow was dead. Knowing Rose's honest nature, I was under no doubt that had she ever had the slightest question mark about my parentage, she would not have hidden it. I therefore drew hope from the fact that she had never questioned that I was anyone other than the son of her dead sister. On the contrary, she had always welcomed me into her life, despite my illegitimate status and all the sordid experiences of my early life. No aunt could have lavished such loving affection on a nephew as she had done me. For that reason the one thing of which I was certain was that I had no desire to speak about Fagin's letter to Rose. For all I knew, the contents of Fagin's letter might be no more than a dead man's wicked lie — a cruel means of rekindling his power over me. How could I possibly risk jeopardizing my relationship with her by disclosing information that might well be false?

Once the first huge shock had worn off, my thoughts turned to how best I should deal with the matter. It was obvious that finding out the truth would be no easy task. Nancy, Bill, Fagin, and Monks were all dead and, as far as I knew, all Fagin's gang had probably long since either been hanged for their criminal activities or else, like the Artful Dodger, been transported to Australia. I had heard nothing of Mr Bumble since that wicked man's loss of status and I had no desire to renew our acquaintance, even if I had the means of discovering his whereabouts, which I did not. Unfortunately Mr Brownlow's death deprived me of the one obvious source that might have known more about what really happened.

I eventually decided that the only person that I could confide in and who might be placed to shed further light on my birth was Mrs Bedwin, even though I had been at first reluctant to involve her. I knew I could trust her completely because she had nursed me in my affliction like a substitute mother, enfolding me in her warmth and natural kindness when many a housekeeper would have acted otherwise. Most women in her position would have advised their master not to take in a child from the gutter. However, Mrs Bedwin had looked at me and seen not a monster but a weak, thin and pallid child so ill-treated as to be near death's door. She had given me not just the physical care required to ensure my survival, but the emotional support that made me want to live. I can recall as if it was yesterday how, once my life was no longer in danger, she carried me downstairs to her own room to sit by her side and how she cried tears of joy at my recovery. Though I tried my best I could not eat all the toasted bread and strong broth she made for me — that would have required a whole workhouse full of starving boys! This was one occasion when Oliver Twist did not require to ask for more.

In some ways recalling those days when Mrs Bedwin had cared for me gave me courage to believe that Fagin's allegations must be wrong. It was in Mrs Bedwin's room that I had first seen the painting of Agnes Fleming. At the time Mrs Bedwin had no idea whom it portrayed. I remember telling her that I felt as if the lady's sorrowful eyes were following me round the room. And then Mr Brownlow was taken aback by the similarity he saw between the portrait and myself. He said the features of Agnes Fleming could be taken as a living copy: the same eyes, the same nose, the same mouth, even the same expression. Mrs Bedwin had endorsed his opinion. More importantly, Monks' obsessive pursuit of my destruction was surely overwhelming proof that the reason for the likeness was that I was indeed Agnes's child. Mr Brownlow had come to have no doubts about my ancestry and I had no doubt myself that Mrs Bedwin shared his certainty. Her love for me had certainly not diminished over the years but had grown ever stronger.

After Mr Brownlow's death it was only her love for her own family that separated us. She had nursed her master through his final illness and then, not without some deliberation because of her affection for me, decided it was time to spend her last days with her son, who had recently returned to London after many years working overseas as a clerk to a merchant in the West Indies. William Bedwin had acquired enough in his years abroad to make a comfortable home for himself and he was keen to care for his mother. Recognizing that she did not like the idea of leaving me alone, he had made it clear that I would always be a welcome person in his home and, needless to say, I had taken up his kind offer and become a regular visitor to their hearth.

Normally I looked forward to seeing Mrs Bedwin, but, on this occasion, despite my hopes that she would somehow prove Fagin to be wrong, I was filled with trepidation. Her son's house was in a reasonably respectable but very overcrowded section of the city. It was an old-fashioned dwelling, darkened by age and smoke and weather. Once standing proud midst open countryside, it was now heavily enclosed by newer and far less attractive buildings, so that not even a blade of grass survived to mark its earlier rural state. Its black and forbidding exterior and the confusing courtyards that now surrounded it did little to commend it, neither at first glance did one's first entrance. Stepping inside the soot-covered house was like moving into its past because its faded furnishings were also almost entirely the product of an earlier age and fashion, except for a few rather incongruous additions that had been acquired throughout her son's years abroad. These were clearly visible because the house was extremely well lit by both candle and fire. Indeed the first action of any bespectacled visitor coming in from the cold was always to wipe their glasses so that they could remove the instant condensation on them.

Any criticism of the house's appearance was soon negated because of the warmth of welcome all entrants received. It put even the heat coming from the large fireplace to shame. Rather like his house, William Bedwin was not a man to be judged by appearances.

40

Outwardly his sallow complexion, grizzled hair and rather grim visage made him appear a gloomy figure, especially as he dressed almost entirely in black. Moreover, years of being subjected to the beck and call of a dictatorial master had left him with a rather haunted look, as if he was never quite sure what demand would be placed on him next. Yet beneath this outward exterior was a generous and warm-hearted man, who delighted in telling a good story and in helping others. He greeted me with all his usual cheer and so too did his mother, though age was now making her visibly frailer each time we met.

After exchanging initial pleasantries, I confided that I had a matter of some concern, which I needed to share with my former nurse. William said he would happily leave us to talk alone because he had to attend to some shopping. Once he was gone, I explained to Mrs Bedwin that I had unexpectedly received a letter written years earlier by Fagin on the eve of his execution and that its contents had deeply troubled me. At the mention of his name her untroubled face clouded over.

'That wicked, sinful wretch. I'm surprised you did not consign the letter unread to the fire. I hope you may not think me uncharitable, for I try to be a good Christian, but I hope its author is still burning in torment in Hell. I see no reason why whatever he has written should not similarly be consumed by flames.'

'You may well be right but what is done cannot be undone. I have read his letter and it is now I who am consumed by torment.'

Her kind face looked with surprise at the intensity of anguish written on my face. She took my hand in hers and urged me to confide in her. Her touch was sufficient to open the floodgates of my heart and, abandoning that stiff upper lip so demanded of a gentleman, I am not ashamed to say I openly wept. Finding it impossible to voice my feelings, I reached into my pocket, and drew out the cursed letter and urged her to read it. This she reluctantly did. I watched as her countenance changed and the tears began to fall. She seemed to age visibly before my eyes as if the burden of what she was reading was cutting away at her remaining strength. I feared I had overburdened her but I had not counted on her strong willpower or the depth of her love for me. As she thrust the document back into my hand so as to rid herself of its hateful touch her face hardened and she gave voice to her anger at its contents:

'How could this disgusting man have treated you so! I knew you had been beaten and I suspected worse, but this confirmation of my fears still hits me hard. Oh, Oliver, Oliver, how much you have suffered and through no fault of your own. This man was a monster and yet he dares to describe his feelings for you as being nothing but love! He knew nothing of love. Unnatural lust is all he felt and, what makes it even worse, he shows no contrition even though he knew when he wrote this that he was about to meet his maker. And to think he must have treated other boys like this over many years. It makes me sick to the stomach. If ever there was a fiend in human form, it is he.'

'But even a fiend can speak truth,' I replied. 'He appears to believe that I am not who you think me to be and never was. Far from being the nephew of Rose Maylie, I am the bastard child of Nancy.'

'I don't believe it. Not for one moment. I can assure you Mr Brownlow had no doubts as to your birth. No doubts whatsoever. Nor did Mr Monks think any other than that you were his relation. This is a wicked, wicked lie, a damned lie.'

'But what about the allegations he makes about Charles Dickens?' I asked.

'How can you believe them to contain a

shred of accuracy? The man is virtually a saint — look at the way he champions the cause of the downtrodden in his novels and exposes all that is hypocritical and wrong with our country. I know Nancy did much that redeemed her, but there is no way such a gentleman would have had a relationship with such a woman. Because Nancy protected you, you sometimes forget her true character and the many crimes she committed. How can you give any of what Fagin says credence? The man never knew the meaning of truthfulness. Talk of some kind of conspiracy to have Nancy killed is simply the wild imaginings of this malevolent creature. None of us liked what happened to her but you must realize that it was no surprise that she should have died brutally at the hands of Bill Sikes. You know yourself that the man was a violent and coarse bully of the very worst kind. Take my advice — burn this foul letter and forget you ever read it. Look to the future, not to an unhappy past.'

Such words brought out all the secret feelings of unworthiness that had for so long marred my life and I answered her in all honesty. 'In my heart I have always known that the unnatural practices I engaged in as a child makes me unworthy of a happy life, so how can I look to the future with anything but foreboding. Nancy should never have died to save my sin-sick soul. You have no idea of the many heinous practices in which I engaged whilst I was Fagin's prisoner. If you did you would never be able to look at me again. All your kindness and affection would turn to dust and ashes and you would shun my presence.'

Mrs Bedwin looked at me in disbelief and horror. 'Oliver, believe me, Nancy died to save you because she, like us, saw that you were an innocent victim. In no way are you in the slightest to blame for what happened in Fagin's den. He alone bears the shame, not you. You were a helpless child forced to commit acts that you know to be wrong. No one can blame you for that, least of all I.'

'But I committed them. They are still my sins.'

'You committed them under duress and with no adult to come to your rescue. Oliver, you must believe me. You were not to blame for anything that passed between you and Fagin or indeed any of his corrupted associates. Whatever happened, you must accept that you are innocent of any guilt. Our dear Lord Jesus looks down on you in loving sorrow, not in anger. His righteous wrath will be confined entirely to the unrepentant man who caused your pain and suffering. Enjoy your life. Think of your position now. You are loved by all who know you — is not that testimony to your good character? And you are now fortunate in having inherited wealth beyond anything that either Mr Brownlow or I once could have dreamed possible. Surely that alone shows that God is now blessing you. Continue using that God-given wealth not only to help others — as I know you have been doing — but to make a good and happy future for yourself.'

As you can imagine, I drew much comfort from her words, but her comment about unexpected wealth puzzled me and so I questioned her. 'Why is my wealth greater than what you or Mr Brownlow expected?'

The change of direction in our conversation troubled her but she was nevertheless quick to reply. 'As you know, Mr Brownlow, foolishly in my opinion, insisted on splitting your rightful inheritance from your father with your wicked half-brother Monks, even though it was not a large estate, it having suffered much from neglect. I know you supported that decision but I did not see then and I do not see now that Monks deserved anything, given his attempt to destroy you. My prediction that Monks would soon squander his part of the inheritance proved accurate. Indeed, the only good outcome of

Mr Brownlow's decision as far as I can see is that Monks's profligate disposal of his inheritance most certainly contributed to his early death. In the light of all this, I regard it as God's blessing on you that Mr Brownlow was able to leave you far more money himself than what came from the reduced estate of your father. Without that you would be far worse off. The reason I talked of greater wealth than Mr Brownlow or I expected is that the dear man acquired much of the money he was able to give you only in recent years. Though he lived comfortably when you first met him, he originally did not have half what he was ultimately able to leave to you.'

'How did he acquire that later wealth?'

'Lord above, I've no idea. I'm a woman and I have no knowledge of business. You'd have to ask his friend Mr Grimwig about that. He may possibly know how my master acquired the wealth he so generously and enthusiastically bequeathed to you. All I know is that you have cause to be grateful for it. I repeat that I have always looked upon it as Heaven's blessing on you that Mr Brownlow acquired the extra money. If you love me, Oliver, take my advice. Accept the blessing of Heaven and forget Fagin and his evil imaginings.'

I might well have taken her advice had not

Mrs Bedwin unwittingly given me cause to doubt whether I really did yet know the truth about myself. I will not bore you with the remainder of our conversation that day. Suffice it to say we parted lovingly. She reiterated her opinion that I was an innocent victim and I promised her that I would not blame myself for the sins of others. What went unsaid was the confusion in my head. I decided I could not voice to her the question that now dominated my thoughts. Could the unexpected wealth that had come Mr Brownlow's way have anything to do with Nancy's murder? If so, then Fagin's letter might not be just the deluded meanderings of an evil man. Before I could relinquish my investigation I felt I had to seek a business meeting with Mr Grimwig, who, you may recall, was the long-standing ex-lawyer friend of my benefactor. I hoped that he would be able to show me that the money came from a source unrelated to me.

It was not a meeting that I looked forward to with any relish. Mr Grimwig was not a man to whom I had ever really taken. That is hardly surprising given the nature of our first meeting. Dressed by Mrs Bedwin in the first suit I had ever worn, I was brought into the room that housed Mr Brownlow's impressive library and there I met Mr Grimwig. As far as he was concerned there were only two sorts of boy — mealy boys and beef-faced boys — and he instantly left me in no doubt that he classed me among the former. When it was explained that I was recovering from a very severe, indeed life-threatening fever, he showed no sympathy. Instead he warned Mr Brownlow against introducing a boy suspected of thieving into his house, saying it was an invitation to have his silver spoons pinched. He said he'd eat his head if I turned out honest and that Mr Brownlow could expect nothing but lies and dishonesty from me. It was Mr Grimwig who also suggested I be given the task of returning some books to a shop — the ill-fated expedition that led to my recapture by Nancy and Bill Sikes. What to me was a catastrophe of the worst possible kind served only to confirm Mr Grimwig in his opinion that I was a thorough-paced little villain — and he still held to that view even when I was subsequently freed.

Mr Brownlow's assertions that his friend's bark was worse than his bite and that Mr Grimwig had a kind nature beneath his gruff exterior never carried much weight with me. Neither did I accept Charles Dickens' take on him. He may have found Mr Grimwig's speech and mannerisms sufficiently amusing to make him depict him as a rather comic figure in his novel about me, but I believe a man who thinks himself always in the right (and who delights in putting down children and criticizing the actions of others) is far from comic. Not surprisingly, I never took much interest in trying to win Mr Grimwig's friendship. We had exchanged only the briefest of conversations at the funeral of Mr Brownlow and I think he must have been very surprised now to receive a request from me to see him. If so, he nevertheless readily acceded, perhaps because, despite all his faults, he had regarded Mr Brownlow with great affection and respect and so felt honour-bound to see the heir to his estate. Or maybe he just wanted to put me in my place again? We arranged to meet at a public house he sometimes frequented, not far from our respective homes. Neutral territory which, I suppose, suited us both.

I will not bother you with an account of where we met for it was a fairly nondescript place. When I entered Mr Grimwig was already ensconced at a table, holding forth as usual about the inadequacies of his fellow men. He was just as I had first met him all those years ago — opinionated and truculent and unsympathetic. He was also one of those men who appears not to change much with the passage of time, even though all around them do. He was just as stout and just as lame as I remembered him and he appeared to be wearing remarkably similar clothes to those he had worn on our first meeting: a blue coat, striped waistcoat, and nankeen breeches and gaiters. He screwed his head to one side as he welcomed me, looking out of the corners of his eyes through a double eyeglass, and uttered the phrase that most peppered his communications with people: 'I'll eat my head, sir, if it isn't Oliver Twist!'

I had already decided that I would not reveal to him anything of the contents of Fagin's letter. I did not think he would share Mrs Bedwin's belief that I was an innocent child corrupted. It was far more likely that he would see in Fagin's account proof that he had always been right in asserting my innate criminality. Before attending the meeting I had concluded that the safest way to see if he knew anything helpful to me was to make him think I was simply seeking some information on my inheritance. This was therefore the line I took.

'Good morning, sir. I am grateful for this opportunity to meet you. We have had our differences in the past but I know you were always a loyal friend to my most kind benefactor. As you are aware, I have inherited all Mr Brownlow's estate.'

'Ay, that you have and against my advice, I might say. I told him I'd eat my head if you didn't waste the money on extravagant living. Bad blood will show and there is no getting away from that.'

'Mr Grimwig, I can assure you that I am not frittering away my inheritance. On the contrary, I have for some time been helping young people escape from the kind of horrors I myself endured. I want to use more of my wealth to help others and it is in that connection that I seek your advice.'

He drank from his tankard and muttered loudly so that all who chose could hear: 'I don't take too kindly to giving help to others. It encourages idleness. Young people should learn to stand on their own feet. I'll eat my head if charity serves any useful purpose. It's all humbug if you ask me.'

I could easily have taken offence at this monstrous statement but instead I ignored his Scrooge-like reply and persevered: 'But you do accept that Mr Brownlow always offered help to others?' He nodded his reluctant assent and I continued: 'I wish to offer most help to causes that might be dear to his heart. Out of modesty he would never speak of whatever causes he chose to help, so I am hoping you can tell me more about his generosity.'

'Then you have come to the wrong place because I never took an interest in his charity work. All I ever advised him on was his business interests — and good advice I gave him.'

'I am sure you did, sir. Perhaps then you could tell me more about his business interests, because that may lead me to give preference to certain causes over others. Sadly I have inherited his money without knowing from whence it came.'

I held my breath. Was this short sentence truly going to be sufficient to lead Mr Grimwig into providing the real information I sought? He looked at me again with that curious parrot-like screwing of his head to one side and eyed me up before speaking. At first he went through what seemed a never-ending stream of minutiae about various minor investments, but then it struck me that he was actually finding it hard to admit that he did not actually know the answer to my question. At last he gave voice to his ignorance, though couching it in terms that protected his arrogance:

'The truth is, you know, your benefactor was never very rich because he too often ignored my advice. He was far too content to be just comfortably well-off and would miss out on calculated risks in the money market. I therefore know as little as you about where his sudden great wealth came from later. If you want more information, you'll have to ask that writer chap, Dickens. I'm pretty sure that it was after some meeting with him that Mr Brownlow acquired his additional wealth. I'll eat my head if these writing fellows don't have access to all kinds of information about investments denied to the likes of us.'

I cannot recall much of our subsequent conversation or even the manner of my departure from the public house. The reference to Dickens's lying behind Mr Brownlow's wealth had my head swimming. Mr Grimwig had unwittingly undone the effects of all Mrs Bedwin's pleas for me to ignore the contents of Fagin's letter. Whatever Mr Grimwig might think, I knew Charles Dickens was no investment adviser. Though the thought was hideous to me, was it therefore possible that my wealth stemmed from my beloved guardian's blackmailing Charles Dickens? And, if so, what was he blackmailing him about? Was it true that Mr Brownlow had known far more about the truth of Nancy's death — and the reason for it — than he had ever told me?

4

Dickens's Story

For several years I had ceased to have any direct contact with the man who had immortalized my childhood. I resented too much what Charles Dickens's writing had done to me and I had no desire to renew our acquaintance. Nevertheless, I had continued to read with immense admiration many of his newspaper articles and most of his subsequent stories and novels. Who could not fail to be entranced by books like *Nicholas Nickleby*, *Martin Chuzzlewit*, *Barnaby Rudge*, and *The Old Curiosity Shop*? Because I wished my past could be put behind me, *A Christmas Carol* held a special place in my affections because it is a tale of a man who manages to relive his past and, in the process, rids himself of past ghosts and changes his future.

I was unsure of what course to take for the first few weeks after my meetings with Mrs Bedwin and Mr Grimwig. During that time I began reading the first instalments of Dickens's latest work, which was a novel called *Dombey And Son*. It will not surprise you to hear that I was one of thousands to be absorbed by its tragic plot, passion and grand style. My sharing in the national concern for the fate of little Paul Dombey made me appreciate once again Dickens's ability to make his audience care for the welfare of the young. He had done the same for Little Nell, Tiny Tim, and many others, as well as for me. It seemed to me that no author could write so forcefully about injustice and not want to see truth revealed. This eventually acted as the necessary trigger to push me into having the courage to visit him in the hope that he could help me to investigate the truth behind what Fagin had written. Nevertheless, it was not without a high degree of anxiety that I begged an audience with the great man.

Whilst he was writing his book about me, Dickens moved from a house in Doughty Street to a larger property in Devonshire Terrace on the corner of Marylebone Road and Marylebone High Street, almost opposite the York Gate that leads into Regent's Park. From the outside it was a respectable but rather plain and dull-looking two-storeyed property. It was marked off from the street by ugly green railings, but I knew these were no barrier to the house having become a general meeting place for men of mark, attracted by the genius who dwelt within. As I knocked for admittance, I knew I was expected and, judging from the tone of his written reply, warmly, but this did not prevent my heart pounding as loudly in my chest as my hand did upon the front door.

I was admitted by one of his servants and led to his study to await him. The thing that struck me most was the way in which he was displaying his relatively newfound wealth throughout the house in its elegant furnishings. Silk damask curtains and silk-covered rosewood chairs vied with brightly coloured floral carpets and attractive candelabra to catch the eye. Equally apparent was his love of books, because rows of them lined large sections of the room. There also seemed to be an excess of mirrors. They were placed all around the room and I wondered whether this reflected a growing if understandable vanity. It was an idea reinforced by his appearance when he entered and greeted me. His attire was highly fashionable. It gave him the air of a dandy, especially as he wore, to my eyes, an excessive amount of jewellery on his hands. However, his manner was far from vain. It was fresh and genial and welcoming. Only the fairly frequent way in which he pulled out his comb to attend to his hair during the course of our meeting betrayed, perhaps, his inherent nervousness at seeing me again.

If the warmth of his greeting immediately recalled our earlier acquaintance, his physical appearance on closer inspection surprised me. He was very different from how I remembered him. Then he had been a charismatic young man, with bright, lively eyes, well-formed facial features, and profuse flowing auburn hair. Now his features bore testimony to the truth of the rumours I had heard. It was commonly stated that he drove himself unreasonably hard and that bouts of manic exertion alternated with periods of deep despair and desperate gloom. Although still not yet forty, he looked far older. His face was heavily lined, his hair had become sparse, and his doorknocker beard was flecked with grey. Only his eyes sparkled with the same youthful vigour.

He expressed his delight at seeing me again and apologized that his recent travels abroad had delayed his responding earlier to my request to meet him. We exchanged the usual pleasantries and he indicated his sorrow at Mr Brownlow's death. He proved a very good listener, drawing out of me my story with his natural ease of manner. I soon forgot that I was in the presence of the country's greatest writer and told him of my life since we had last met as if he was a close friend. He stood with his hands in his trouser pockets and threw his head slightly back, his eyes gleaming with infectious warmth which conveyed both good humour and human concern, depending on the drift of my tale. He vowed he had no knowledge of how Mr Brownlow had acquired greater wealth in recent years and made my suspicion that it might have anything to do with him seem ludicrous. However, on hearing my account of Fagin's letter, the warmth of his initial welcome frosted over and I thought he was going to dismiss me instantly from his presence. Fortunately, after a moment's hesitation, he seemed to think again. Whether he feared I might begin investigating elsewhere or whether he decided he owed me a degree of honesty I do not know, but he volunteered to tell me as much of the truth as he knew about Nancy and her death.

Everyone who met Dickens was always captivated by his ability to tell stories and I believe on this occasion he excelled himself. He spoke in a sharp, jerky but engaging way, with not a touch of affectation or pomposity. I listened, awestruck by the intimacy of his confession. Even now, I can repeat almost every word he said and recall virtually every gesture he made. And so I cannot do better than repeat his account exactly as he told it to me, even though I cannot convey the wonderful and quickly changing expressions of his face throughout his lengthy discourse.

'I promise to tell you the truth, Mr Twist, and this is the truth, not just as it was but as I still feel it. I may be famous and successful and happy now, but once my whole nature was permeated with the grief and humiliation of being an abandoned and ill-used child. When I first heard your story, I knew I had to write about it because in part it felt so like mine. The loneliness that was so much part of your childhood was also a prominent feature in mine, as was the degradation. Forgive me, but I must explain my own background if you are to understand. All I ask is that you do not make use of the information to harm my family or me.

'My father was as kind-hearted and generous a man as ever lived in the world and my first memories of childhood are all happy ones. At first it was easy for me to grow up imagining that I would become a learned and distinguished man, but, when my family returned to London from Chatham, it appeared as if all those hopes would be dashed forever. The area in which we came to live in Camden Town was still semi-rural but that did not prevent our new house being shabby, dingy, damp and mean. Despite the air of decay, our neighbours sought to disguise their poverty in a desperate attempt to keep up appearances. It may sound ludicrous but the more genteel among them, in answering knocks on their doors, endeavoured to admit their visitors whilst keeping out of sight behind the door so as to give the impression it had been opened by a servant. I recall how the same desire to maintain appearances meant that a working bookbinder was looked down upon by his neighbours for keeping fowls and so lowering the tone. Signboards and placards declaring rooms for let were discouraged. A few houses were considered a disgrace to us all when they were afflicted in their lower extremities with eruptions of mangling and clear starching because their residents were reduced to taking in washing.

'Despite the pretensions of my family and the other residents, there was a debt collector who used to come to the area so regularly to deliver the summonses for rates and taxes that you might have supposed he was delivering circulars. My father never paid anything until the last extremity, and heaven knows how he paid it then. Although he never undertook any business without applying himself zealously, conscientiously, punctually, and honourably, his financial affairs were increasingly shaky. As I grew older this made him seem to lose all idea of educating me, although I was a child of singular abilities, quick, eager, delicate, and easily hurt. No one else in my family, not even my mother, suggested that something might be spared from our meagre income to send me to a school. My parents would care for me night and day whenever I was sick, but the rest of the time I was either ignored or expected to clean people's shoes and do other small chores around the unattractive rooms we rented.

'Occasionally a family's hunger must be allayed even at the cost of one's self-respect and so I would be sent on an errand to pawn some of our ever-diminishing possessions. I still recall with a sense of shame how furtively I used to skulk around the pawnshops, glancing timorously and irresolutely at the golden balls outside their premises, trying to guess which one might be the more generous. These dirty shops contained the most extraordinary and confused jumble of old, worn-out, wretched articles that can ever be imagined. My wonderment that some of them had ever been bought was matched only by my astonishment at the idea that any of them might ever be sold again! Odd volumes from sets of little-read books, wineglasses of different patterns, pans full of rusty keys, gaudy chimney ornaments — cracked, of course, pickle jars without stoppers, high-backed chairs with spinal complaints and wasted legs, wearing apparel and bedding, fenders and fire-irons; indeed a miscellany of objects of every description. Even the supposed special items, such as an unframed portrait of some lady who had flourished in a previous century, by an artist who never flourished at all, were to my eye unattractive. And the clothes in such establishments told the saddest tale. The make and materials of these shoddy items, so carelessly heaped together, spoke of better days; and the older they were, the greater the misery and destitution of those whom they once adorned.

'I sometimes wandered into areas less salubrious than the one where I lived but I hated it if I misjudged the time and this led to me being out when night fell. Then the great city lay outstretched before me like a dark shadow on the ground, reddening the sluggish air with a deep dull light, that told of a labyrinth of public ways and shops, and swarms of busy people. Long lines of poorly lighted streets might be faintly traced, with here and there a brighter spot. But these merely revealed the piles of uneven roofs oppressed by chimneys and the occasional tall steeple looming in the air. Once-noble buildings were here reduced to squalid tenements, their sewage flowing into the street. Like you, I soon came to know that in every overcrowded room men, women and children lived in indescribable filth with cleanliness a thing unknown. I have known — as of course have you — yards and cellars so full of human excrement that I could scarcely cross them without befouling myself.

'I remember one evening when the cold, thin rain, which had been drizzling all day, began to pour in earnest. The rustling of umbrellas and the constant clicking of shoes on the slippery and uneven cobbles bore testimony to the inclemency of the weather. As the crowds, which had been passing to and fro throughout the day, dwindled away and the little ragged boys who usually disported themselves about the streets, stood crouched in little knots under projecting doorways, only the noise of shouting and quarrelling in the public houses broke the melancholy stillness. I saw a wretched woman with a mewling infant in her arms. Round its meagre form she carefully wrapped the remnant of her own scanty shawl, whilst attempting to sing a popular ballad in the hope of obtaining a few pence from any compassionate passer-by. A brutal laugh at her weak voice was all she gained. The tears fell thick and fast down her pale oval face. The child was cold and hungry, and its low half-stifled wailing added to her misery as she moaned aloud and sank despairingly down on a cold, damp doorstep. I knew they were both doomed to die of cold and hunger and that no one cared. Nor would anyone care for me if ever I were reduced to such a condition.

'With such experiences the joys of childhood were denied me. I fell into a state of dire neglect, the memory of which still haunts me. I suffered very much from other boys who chased me down turnings, brought me to bay in doorways, and treated me quite savagely, though I am sure I gave them no offence. To add insult to my unhappy condition, my parents, though denying me any schooling, chose to send my sister Fanny to the Royal Academy of Music. What would I have given, if I had had anything to give, to have been sent to any place of education? My mind craved to be taught something and I did not care where. I was prepared to accept any school, however humble. I could not understand why my sister was so favoured and I was so ignored.

'My mother came up with the grand idea of supplementing the family income by opening a school for young ladies and I was given the task of posting advertisements for it through letterboxes. Nobody ever came to it and I cannot recollect that anybody ever proposed to come, or even that preparation was made to receive anybody. Our visitors therefore were not clients but more debt collectors, because my father continued to squander what little resources we had. I still remember how one dirty-faced man, I think he was a bootmaker, used to edge himself into the passageway of the house as early as seven o'clock in the morning and call upstairs to my father: 'Come! You aren't out yet, you know. Pay us, will you? Don't hide, you know, that's mean. I wouldn't be mean if I was you'. But, Mr Twist, our whole life had become mean. Mean and shabby and dismal.

'Not surprisingly, I kept myself apart from others of my own age and I became a desperately lonely young boy. Books became my only comfort and I read the few we owned over and over again. They called me an odd child and perhaps I was, but it was an oddity born of isolation. It was always a relief when I had the chance to visit my godfather, who alone seemed to take some interest in me. He was a sail-maker and ships' chandler who lived in Church Row, just behind the great church of Nicholas Hawksmoor in Limehouse. I used to pass

all the boat-building yards where the very air was perfumed with wood chips and I saw all trades swallowed up in mast, oar and block-making. It used to remind me of happier days when I was five and six, growing up in Chatham. I dreamt of boarding a boat and sailing down the stench-ridden Thames to freedom and a new life in countries where opportunities would abound and my childhood hopes of future greatness could be rekindled.

'In reality my troubles were only just beginning because far worse lay ahead of me. A friend of my father had become the manager of a boot blacking company and he suggested to my impoverished parents I should start working there at a salary of six or seven shillings a week. To my horror they rapidly assented and, just two days after my twelfth birthday, I set off for a three-mile walk from Camden Town to the Strand to commence my new career. The company was based in a warehouse in an impoverished area, which was an unwholesome maze of squalid corners and filthy alleys. 'Warren's Blacking', as it was called, operated in a crazy, tumbledown old house on the left hand side of the way at old Hungerford Stairs, abutting the river and overrun with rats. I just have to shut my eyes and I can still see its

wainscoted rooms and worm-eaten, damp, and rotten floors and staircase. I can still hear the sound of the grey rats as they swarmed down below in the cellars and scuffled and squeaked their way up the staircase into the place where we worked. I can still smell the stinking river water that lapped around this God-forsaken manufactory, carrying, amid its unending filth and flotsam, the occasional bloated corpse, the tragic outcome of some suicide or accident or maybe the decomposing evidence of yet another of this city's unsolved crimes.

'My task in this stinking hellhole was to take bottles of blacking and prepare them for sale by covering the pots with a piece of oilpaper and then a piece of blue paper. I would tie each bottle with string and paste on a printed label. And I did that for ten hours a day, my whole being racked with the humiliation of it. My meagre earnings did not prevent my father being declared an insolvent. He was incarcerated in the Marshalsea Prison. My heart felt it would break when I visited him there for the first time and he told me the sun had set upon him for ever and that he would spend the rest of his life in that dank, malodorous, soul-destroying place, where the very stones exuded despair. His eyes awash with tears, he told me to

remember that if a man had twenty pounds a year and spent nineteen pounds, nineteen shillings, and sixpence of it, the result would be happiness, but, if he spent a shilling more, he would be doomed to wretchedness. It was good advice but I regret to say he never heeded it himself. Almost everything, by degrees, was sold or pawned and my mother and the rest of my family had soon to join him there.

'Can you imagine what it is like to see your parents pent up in a narrow prison cell and watch their faces gradually assume that squalid and sickly hue which marks every person deprived of light and freedom? Whenever I visited I was forced to listen to the screams and cries of those around them till I wept for the sheer futility of their existence. And my life outside was not much better. It seemed just a larger prison in which the walls of massed humanity threatened to squeeze the very life out of me. I lived in horrible lodgings, surrounded by the equally impoverished. All around me were signs of want and destitution: emaciated faces, stick-like limbs, threadbare coats and trousers, moth-eaten gowns and damp shawls. In this harsh world, I might just be twelve but I had to win my own food. I kept a small loaf of bread and a quarter of pound of cheese on a shelf in my squalid garret room and this was my main meal each night when I returned from my labours in the warehouse. For month after month I had no advice, no counsel, no encouragement, no consolation, no support, from anyone that I can call to mind.

'I prayed to be lifted out of the humiliation and neglect in which I was abandoned, but no one heard my prayers. When I heard that my sister, who was still at the Academy, had been awarded a silver medal for her studies, the tears ran down my face. I felt as if my heart was rent. I could not bear to think of myself being beyond the reach of all such honourable ambition and success. In my desperation I turned increasingly for companionship to the two boys who worked alongside me, Bob Fagin and Paul Green. Bob was an orphan and Paul the son of a fireman employed at Drury Lane Theatre. Both were very different from me in terms of their birth and attitude and they were old beyond their years, using language that was coarse and vulgar. They regarded me as 'the young gentleman' and laughed at my inexperience and naïvety. Since my arrival I had been careful not to tell them how I came to be there or how much I hated it. Instead I had won their interest by regaling them with some of the stories I had read and, if there was no one watching us, occasionally acting them out. Even if your heart is breaking, playing the clown can sometimes be the only means of self-preservation.

'Bob and Paul invited me to 'experience life'. In my desperate desire for friendship, I responded, accompanying them to those low quarters of the city I had hitherto avoided. There I freely observed every vice you care to name and many I would not wish to mouth. I saw prodigies of wickedness, want, and beggary. I saw every kind of theft. I saw gangs reduce their victims to bloody pulp. I saw whores giving their bodies to drunks in the street for all to watch. I learnt just how much poverty can corrupt and destitution distort and I was deeply ashamed of my newly acquired knowledge, even if I knew myself to be not only the son of an insolvent but also the grandson of an embezzler.

'One dark night a few weeks after my thirteenth birthday, I became not just an observer but also an unwilling participant. Bob and Paul, recognizing those changes in me which marked that I was becoming a man, took me to the house of Bob's uncle. I suspect it had once been a house of some distinction but it was in terminal decline, a dirty den of a place. Its panelled walls were black with neglect and dust and most of its mouldering shutters were fast closed, the bars that held them screwed tight into the discoloured wood. This made the rat-infested rooms dark and gloomy, despite the efforts of their mostly drunken inmates to give the house an air of festivity. Plenty of alcohol and the services of a few hard-eyed but full-bosomed women were its only attractions. Bob and Paul encouraged me to drink more than I had ever done before and then handed me over to one of the youngest of the prostitutes present. I will not dwell on the sordid details, Mr Twist, but they and others far worse than them enjoyed watching as she took my final innocence away.

'And that, believe it or not, was my introduction to Nancy. She was scarce older than me but she was a corrupt product of a system that no writer, however great, is allowed to fully expose. Our society likes even its moral crusaders to avoid certain topics. It prefers to pretend that this is a Christian society, turning a blind eye to the little creatures in petticoats that pursue men in the streets, plucking at their garments and seeking to entice them into sex by making lewd suggestions. The law may say it's illegal to have sex with a child under the age of twelve but you know as well as I do that it does nothing to prevent child prostitution. Nancy may have had the face of an angel, but her experiences of indiscriminate sexuality had given her the heart of a devil. I guess her seduction of me — if you can call her rape of me that — was just a momentary diversion from the old men she was normally asked to favour with her lascivious attentions. It gave me no pleasure and I doubt if she thought much of my childish masculinity.

'The next day the full implication of what had happened to me struck home. I cannot describe to you how common and dirty I felt. At work, when Bob and Paul began to taunt me with what had happened, I was taken with a seizure. They had to lay me down on the straw-strewn floor as the spasms shook me. Bob filled empty blacking bottles with hot water and tried to apply them to my icy body. I writhed on the floor in my anguish.'

Charles Dickens paused, his ashen face contorted with the pain of what he had just revealed to me. Even after so many years I could see that the depraved nature of the events he had recounted were an agony to recall. He moved across the room and poured himself a drink. His hand trembled as he brought the glass to his lips. He quickly poured himself another and speedily drank that also. I asked him if he felt able to continue. He turned and nodded, whispering through his gritted teeth, 'The worst is yet to come.'

5

Murder Most Foul

By a Herculean effort Dickens composed himself and, having collected his thoughts, resumed his story. My pen cannot describe the anguish that swept across his face at intervals. To me it was obvious that his was a tale written in his very blood:

'They say every cloud has a silver lining and my illness gave me the excuse I needed to avoid further expeditions with Bob and Paul and, a few weeks later, my time at the factory ended. The company moved to new premises near Covent Garden and my father, who had secured release from prison, came to watch me at work through the new shop window. I think it was only then that the degradation of my situation struck home because he immediately quarrelled with my cousin and took me away, despite the protests of my uncaring mother that the family needed my earnings. I never shall forget or forgive that my mother was keen to keep me there. It may seem a harsh thing to say, but I still feel my entire family still looks upon me as something to be plucked and torn to pieces for their advantage. I fear they have no idea of, and no care for, my existence in any other light. And, I'll be honest with you, Mr Twist, there are times when my soul sickens at the sight of them.

'I foolishly thought that I could put my experiences with Bob and Paul and, above all, with Nancy, behind me. My father enrolled me at a school called Wellington House Academy and there I worked hard to educate myself, even though its respected proprietor was by far the most ignorant and worst-tempered man that it has ever been my misfortune to know. He saw the teaching profession not as a vocation but as a business in which the aim was to make as much as he could from us and to put into teaching us as little effort as possible. His main expertise lay in corporal punishment. He was always smiting the palms of offenders with some diabolical instrument, or viciously drawing a pair of pantaloons tight with one of his large hands, and caning the wearer with the other. I'm sure hitting us boys was the principal solace of his existence.

'What we learnt largely came from the school's usher. He was our writing master, mathematical master, and English master, and he also made out the bills, mended the pens, and did all sorts of other things. Sometimes he was assisted by our Latin master, a colourless, doubled-up, near-sighted man with a crutch. He was always telling us he was cold and he used to disclose the ends of flannel under all his garments. He kept applying a ball of pocket-handkerchief to some part of his face with a screwing action round and round and he had the bizarre habit of putting onions into his ears in the mistaken belief that this helped to reduce his deafness. Nevertheless, this poor man was a good scholar and he took great pains when he saw (as he did in me) intelligence and a desire to learn. There was also a French master, who used to come in the sunniest weather with a handleless umbrella, and a fat little dancing master who used to come in a gig, and teach hornpipes to the more advanced among us, though to what advantage I can scarce surmise.

'Most of my fellow students took comfort in possessing pets in the form of red-polls, linnets, canaries, and, the favourite of all, white mice. They trained their mice far better than the teachers trained us. I recall one white mouse, who lived in the covers of a Latin dictionary and who ran up ladders, drew Roman chariots, shouldered muskets, and turned wheels. He might have achieved greater things, but for having the misfortune to mistake his way in a triumphal procession, when he fell into a deep inkstand, was dyed black and drowned. Amid such scenes of boyish fun, I was very conscious of having passed through scenes of which my classmates could have no knowledge, and of having acquired experiences foreign to my age and appearance. There were times when I felt it was an imposture to go there as an ordinary schoolboy. Nevertheless, I won prizes and great fame and I was assured that I was a clever boy.

'Two years later my father's continued inability to control the family's finances forced me to leave. I took up a post as a junior clerk in the office of Ellis and Blackmore in Holborn Court. There I worked for eighteen months, using every moment of my limited spare time to learn shorthand so that I could become a reporter both of court proceedings and parliamentary debates. I was determined to have a job in which I was my own master, even if it meant struggling to make ends meet. Whatever I have tried to do in life, I have tried to do well. Believe me, Mr Twist, there is no substitute for thoroughgoing, ardent and sincere determination combined with hard work. I did not allow my resolution to cool. It was one of the irons I kept hot, and hammered at with a perseverance I may honestly admire.

'I became a reporter for the *Mirror of Parliament*, a newspaper run by one of my uncles. Most of the time the debates I listened to in the Commons and Lords were excruciatingly boring, a mixture of noise and confusion and pointless point-scoring. I used to observe the Members of Parliament going out and coming in, all talking, laughing, lounging, coughing, questioning, or groaning. They presented a conglomeration of confusion and conflict to be met with nowhere else, not even excepting Smithfield on a market day, or a cockpit in its glory. Night after night I recorded predictions that never came to pass, professions of action that were never fulfilled, explanations that were only meant to mystify rather than to clarify. I wallowed in nothing but words, working incredibly long hours. I drank coffee by the gallon to keep myself awake. With all the determination and energy of an eighteen-year-old, I was determined to make this just the step to a better career.

'It was at this demanding time of my budding career that I found the romance which my brief and humiliating sexual contact with Nancy had so patently lacked. I fell desperately in love with the dark-eyed daughter of a banker. Her name was Maria Beadnell. If I say she was a picture of sweet loveliness, I do a disservice to her manifold charms. I was swallowed up in an abyss of love for her. Though I often was exhausted from my reporting, I would still walk in the early hours of the morning from the House of Commons to Lombard Street just to look at the house in which she slept. Oh, what fools love makes of us! For three years I swore every possible form of blind devotion and redoubled my efforts to achieve a career worthy of her. I loved her with the most extraordinary earnestness and I held volumes of imaginary conversations with her mother on the subject of our union. Believe me, you cannot overrate the strength of my feeling at that time. I would have died for her with the greatest alacrity! There never was such a poor and devoted fellow as I was.

'Unfortunately her parents remained unimpressed by either my prospects or my efforts. Although I rose to become a reporter for the more prestigious *Morning Chronicle*, they ensured that the courtship ended in failure. Now that I am so successful, Mr Twist, I suspect they have lived to regret their actions. If so, I am pleased, because at the time no parents seemed crueller. My immediate response to their hostility and Maria's rejection of my suit was to seek oblivion in drink but that only made me more wretched. So I plunged myself into new challenges, writing not only reports for the *Morning Chronicle* but also stories and articles for an offshoot paper, the unimaginatively named *Evening Chronicle*. Thus I moved seamlessly from reporter to writer and I assumed in the latter role the pen name of 'Boz', which was the nickname of one of my younger brothers. Looking back, my early stories were crude and ill considered, and they bear obvious marks of haste and inexperience, but at the time I was delighted because they were very leniently and favourably received on their first appearance.

'I soon found myself moving in new circles and, in particular, I became a regular visitor to the home of my newspaper boss, George Hogarth, who had been one of the most eminent among the literati of Edinburgh and an intimate companion of Sir Walter Scott. I basked in the attention of his four pretty daughters, Catherine, Mary, Georgina, and Helen. The society of young girls is a very delightful thing and I gave myself freely to their entertainment and they to mine. I came to see in the eldest, Catherine, every quality that Maria had lacked. Although outwardly not as pretty as my former love, Catherine had every inward virtue that Maria had failed to possess. She was amiable and unassuming, generous and eager to please. She won my affection and I offered to marry her. She accepted and my writing proved as successful as my engagement. The public had taken *Sketches by Boz* to their hearts so I was asked to produce a more ambitious set of stories. At the very end of March in the year 1836 the first episode of my *Pickwick Papers* appeared in print. My powers of invention seemed to know no bounds. Do you know, Mr Twist, that, over the course of the next eighteen months or so, I created no less than eight hundred and sixty-five characters around Pickwick and set his adventures in almost one hundred and seventy different places?'

I nodded. 'It is, indeed, a vastly entertaining book, sir, and one I have read with pleasure more than once.'

Dickens acknowledged my praise with a smile. 'Yes, indeed, I was convinced I had freed myself from the past and all its heartaches and that my good fortune was secured. I obtained a special marriage licence in order to marry Catherine, even though she was still a minor. We set up our first home in a small three-roomed flat at Furnival's Inn, and shortly afterwards Catherine announced I would become a father. My joy seemed complete. I shall never be so happy again as I was in those chambers. Though they were only three storeys high, I felt I had ascended to the entrance to Heaven itself. However, I did not realize that a serpent had already entered my Garden of Eden. Unbeknown to me, Nancy had come back into my life and she was about to make her presence felt again.

'The previous autumn I had been writing some stories on prison life and, as part of my research, I had gone to Newgate Prison. I detest this gloomy depository of the guilt and misery of London. Its rough heavy walls, small grated windows, and low massive doors look as if they were made for the express purpose of letting people in and never letting them out again. The throngs of wretched inmates, bound and helpless, know that within a few yards of their dismal cells the outside world passes them by, one perpetual stream of life and bustle. Those condemned to die are endlessly tortured by having to listen hour by hour and day by day to the light laugh and merry whistle of those who are free.

'I delivered my credentials to the slovenly servant who answered my knock at the governor's house. I was ushered into a little office, which had two windows that both looked into the Old Bailey. It was fitted up like an ordinary attorney's office and contained a wainscoted partition, a shelf or two, an almanac, a clock, and a couple of stools on which perched a pair of clerks, dressed all in black. After a slight delay my guide arrived, a respectable looking man in his early fifties. He was also dressed entirely in black and he wore a broad-brimmed hat, which obscured much of his face. He led me through a couple of rooms to a door which opened on to a square, which itself led off into several paved yards. In these unhappy places the prisoners take such air and exercise as is permitted to them. After passing through what seemed an endless number of gates, each of which had to be unlocked and then relocked, we came to a door composed of thick bars of wood, through which were discernible, passing to and fro in a narrow yard, some twenty women. Most, as soon as they were aware of my presence, retreated to their cells. I discovered that one side of the yard was railed off into a kind of iron cage, less than six feet high and roofed at the top. Only within its confines were female prisoners permitted to communicate with any visitor.

'Two or three women were standing at different parts of the grating, conversing with family or friends, although a very large proportion of the prisoners appeared to have no one at all. Some inmates and visitors were prepared to speak about their lives to me. The others' stories I surmised. I particularly remember one visitor — a yellow, haggard, decrepit old woman, dressed in a tattered gown which had once been a wholesome red but was now terribly faded and begrimed with indescribable filth. She clutched in her hands the remains of an old straw bonnet, with the remnants of a red ribbon. The personification of misery and destitution, she pleaded with a good-looking, robust female inmate, whose most prominent feature was her profusion of golden hair, which shook gently in the wind. This daughter, for such I took her to be, was unmoved by her mother's entreaties. She appeared hardened beyond all hope of redemption and only showed interest when given the few halfpence, which her miserable parent had brought, ill though she could afford them.

'Whilst I observed this scene and others I was, unbeknown to me, also being watched. I had been seen and recognized by Nancy, who happened to be visiting one of Newgate's inmates. Nancy never forgot a face and she quickly recognized in me the naïve boy whom she had seduced, though at first she could not remember my name. She asked her associate if she knew who I was. She was told my name and that I was a respected writer and reporter for the press. However, she chose not to make herself known to me at the time and so I passed on to see more of the prison, including a similar yard for men, completely oblivious of what momentous events would stem from her having seen me. Looking back, I suspect she wanted time to investigate my career before speaking to me. I think it highly likely that she planned to try her hand at a little blackmail when the opportunity arose. If that was the case, your arrival at Fagin's a year later put other ideas into her head about the use she could make of me.

'One night towards the end of November 1836 I was making my way to the Hogarth's house when Nancy approached me and begged for my assistance. I have to confess my immediate horror at seeing her again soon turned to fascination. She was, as you know, bewitchingly beautiful and her lively mind and infectious wit set her far above most of her peers. I was looking for a new idea for my next book because even my invention for fresh adventures about Pickwick was beginning to dry up. Nancy acted the role of Scheherazade to my need for a good story. She informed me she had a tale that would make people sit up and listen and she began to unfold the misadventures of a workhouse orphan called Oliver Twist and the terrible life he had led. I was immediately hooked. I sensed the potential in her account, and she knew it. The government had recently introduced significant changes in the Poor Law and the nature of life in the workhouse was a very topical issue.

'Telling me more of your story became Nancy's perfect excuse for securing further meetings with me, during which she exerted all her not inconsiderable charm. I foolishly did not see the dangers into which this would lead me. At that time fiction frequently pretended that the criminal was a kind of hero. Highwaymen, for example, were depicted as seductive fellows, amiable for the most part, faultless in dress, plump in pocket, choice in horseflesh, bold in bearing, fortunate in gallantry. They were fit companions for the bravest. I had no desire to write of such romantic highwaymen or moonlit heaths with merrymaking in the snuggest of taverns. Instead I wanted to depict the cold, wet, shelterless midnight streets of London and the foul and frowsty dens in which hunger and disease dwell as the handmaids of crime and the destroyers of innocence. I wanted to portray thieves as they really are in the world which

Nancy and I knew. I wanted to describe Fagin and his gang in all their deformity, in all their wretchedness, in all the squalid misery of their lives, forever skulking uneasily through the dirtiest paths of life.

'I readily agreed to become a participant in your rescue from the clutches of those who had abused my own innocence and who were abusing yours. You know the details of how this was achieved. I then embarked on the serialization of your story in the February of 1837. By then my meetings with Nancy were becoming more difficult, despite the fact we had managed to remove you from Fagin's control. I made the mistake of telling her how happy my life had become and, for reasons that I failed to understand, she became increasingly jealous of my relationship with my wife once Catherine gave birth to our first son, whom we christened Charles. She seemed to think that you, Oliver, united her and me in a way that was deeper and more significant than anything I shared with Catherine.

'I soon realized that she thought any child born to me would somehow rebound upon my willingness to continue helping you. My defence of my wife — and I confess I foolishly compared her virtue with Nancy's fallen state — seemed to send Nancy into a paroxysm of fury. She launched into such an obscene vocal attack on her that even now I cannot bring myself to repeat a word of it. She vowed to make Catherine pay for casting such a spell over me. To my undying regret I naïvely laughed at her curses and ignored her threats.

'On the evening of 6 May, a date engraven forever on my memory, I went to the St James's Theatre with my wife and her younger sister, Mary. She was staying with us in order to help Catherine following the birth of our son. The performance was a farce called *Is She His Wife?* which I had written. I was understandably very excited at the prospect of seeing my own writing, whatever its imperfections, being performed because I had long had a fascination with matters theatrical. Even as a child I used to go alone to see shows and, if challenged, I would pretend to look for somebody as if I had been inadvertently separated from the adult who had brought me. The theatre offered a different reality from the one I knew and I welcomed all its sham.

'Imagine my horror, then, when Nancy intercepted us just as we were about to enter the theatre. She was acting as if she was a street-seller and was offering for sale some brandy-balls made of sugar, water, peppermint, and a little cinnamon. Knowing that the sale of sweets was far from her normal occupation, I was understandably suspicious of her motives. I tried to get Catherine and Mary to ignore her but my kind-hearted wife and sister-in-law would have none of my interference. Beguiled by her charm, they determined to buy some of her sweets and they criticized me for my unkindness to a poor woman who was simply trying to make an honest living. I managed to draw Catherine away but Mary talked further with Nancy and, to my frustration, I could not hear what was whispered between them because of the noise of the crowd around us. To my relief Nancy seemed content with the snatched conversation and did not press herself any further on our company. Mary also appeared untroubled by whatever had been said and we all enjoyed the show.

'I thought no more of the matter until our return home at about one in the morning. My sister-in-law went to her room but, before she could undress, she gave a heart-rending cry and collapsed. We hurriedly called a doctor. He declared it was a problem with Mary's heart. We applied every remedy that his skill and our anxiety could suggest. She seemed eventually to rally after a bout of being repeatedly sick and she managed to swallow a little brandy from my hand. She then entered into a calm and gentle sleep as I held her in my arms and I thought the crisis was past. It was some time before I realized that the body I held so lovingly had — without my being aware — breathed its last. I was merely holding her lifeless form whilst her soul had fled to Heaven. It pains me still that the very last words she whispered were of the love she felt for her sister and me.

'Everyone who knew Mary loved her. She was one of God's angels both in her looks and in her temperament. From the day of our marriage the dear girl had been the grace and life of our home, our constant companion, and the sharer of all our little pleasures. Her death tore my newfound happiness apart. I was so shaken and unnerved by the loss of this dear girl that I was compelled for once to give up all idea of monthly work and to seek rest and quiet. As if being deprived of her sunshine was insufficient punishment, other calamities followed. First, my mother-in-law collapsed. Then, far worse, my wife, who had become pregnant again, suffered a miscarriage. And, through all this I hid from the world my conviction that Nancy had murdered my sister-in-law. I was sure the sweets had been poisoned and that their intended victim had been Catherine, but I had no proof — the remaining sweets had been thrown away before we left the theatre — and I was ashamed of owning up to my acquaintance with a whore.

'People say I was overwhelmed with grief at Mary's death to an unhealthy extent, but now you know the true reason for my despair. I had unwittingly brought a mild, gentle, and beautiful seventeen-year-old innocent into fatal contact with a woman drawn from one of the darkest hellholes in London. I could hardly sleep because Mary haunted my dreams, sometimes bearing in her arms the bloody corpse of my wife's aborted child. I vowed vengeance on Nancy and I knew how to wreak it. It was a simple matter to let Fagin know of all the secrets she had betrayed. I knew I could count on him to see she was dealt with. You know the outcome. He told Bill Sikes, who was never a man to tolerate such an act of duplicity. The outcome was a foregone conclusion. Bill battered her to death. I was responsible for the murder of a whore and a murderess and, may God forgive me, I still rejoice in her death and the manner of it. In my imaginings I sometimes feel that I am Sikes, that it is my hands that wield the repeated blows on her skull. And I tell you, Mr Twist, each hammer blow is my revenge for Mary's untimely death.

'I have avoided you because you remind me

too much of that unhappy time of my life and because Nancy's death failed to free me from my sense of failure at allowing my sister-in-law to be murdered. Indeed, if truth be told, it was Mary's haunting face that gave such power to my description of the death of Little Nell in *The Old Curiosity Shop*. When my account threw the nation into mourning, only I knew they mourned fiction whilst I mourned fact. Speak to my friends and they will tell you I grew so wretched at the horrible shadow this cast over me that it was as much as I could do to go on living. So strange did my behaviour become that there were rumours that I had become an alcoholic or had passed into madness.

'For a time I contemplated moving to America because so many places here remind me daily of her loss. I travelled there, but I found it not to be the land of liberty and liberalism I had expected. I soon yearned after our English customs and manners, especially disliking the American propensity to spit everywhere. Whenever I journeyed on a train, the flashes of saliva flew so perpetually and incessantly out of the windows all along the way that it looked as if they were ripping open feather-beds inside, and letting the wind dispose of their feathers!

'And, though I found Americans to be

earnest, hospitable, kind, frank, enthusiastic, and far less prejudiced than you would suppose, I tired of the crowds that besieged me wherever I went. If I walked in the street, I was followed by a multitude. If I stayed at home, the house became, with callers, like a fair. If I went to a party, I was so enclosed and hemmed about by people, that, stand where I might, I was exhausted for want of air. Whenever I dined, I had to talk about everything to everybody. I couldn't even drink a glass of water without having a hundred people looking down my throat when I opened my mouth to swallow. I became an object rather than a person and I never knew less of myself in all my life, or had less time for those confidential interviews with myself, whereby I earn my bread.

'When I returned I found that the sweetness of my literary success, like my marriage, was still regularly soured by my unhappy memories of Mary's loss. I foolishly pursued a girl called Catherine Weller, simply because she resembled Mary, but, fortunately, her marriage to another man pulled me to my senses. I dabbled with the occult, attending a seance and trying the art of table spinning to see if I could communicate with my dead sister-in-law. It is no coincidence that ghosts feature in some of my tales for there are times when I feel I live in the land of shadows. In my recent travels abroad I found, God forgive me, that the many churches dedicated to the Virgin Mother caused me to think too much of my lost Mary. So do not be surprised when I tell you that, since writing your story, I have avoided the danger of mixing too much fact with my fiction and risking further tragedy. Although many of my characters are still based on the people I meet, the situations I place them in are now mostly all my invention.

'With all this in mind I suggest, Mr Twist, that you do not invent a story where there is none. Do not mistake short-lived shadows for realities. I do not know how Mr Brownlow came to be able to leave you so much money but enjoy your good fortune. It is possible that Nancy believed you to be her son, but Fagin's allegations about there being some dark secret about your birth which I needed to hide are but the sick and demented ravings of a man about to face the gallows. The truth is much simpler. Nancy brought me nothing but grief. She raped me when I was but a child of thirteen and killed one of the dearest persons in the world. I live in the constant shadow of her cruelty. If I were you I would not wish to discover any links with a woman so debased. Believe me, Mr Twist, stick to the family you have acquired. Who would want the foul Nancy as their mother?'

I found it difficult to know how to respond to Dickens' final words, which seemed more of a challenge than a question. We both appeared to recognize there was little more to be said. The emotion with which he had told his tale had left both him and me feeling drained and exhausted. I thanked him for his painful honesty and we exchanged a few brief comments about what had happened to others connected with my early life. He appeared to know little about most of them and to care still less. We said we ought to meet each other again but neither of us expected to do so. I now knew why he had avoided me and, for my part, I had no desire to continue our renewed acquaintance. I cursed the day I had opened Fagin's letter. If Nancy really was the child-seducing murderess Dickens believed her to be, my connection with her was indeed most undesirable. I bade him farewell and he bid me good day.

6

The House of Fallen Women

After the immediate shock of Charles Dickens's revelations wore off I found myself questioning his account of events and wondering whether he was simply manipulating me. When he challenged me as to why anyone would want a whore and a murderess as a parent, he fully understood that I had long regarded Agnes Fleming as my mother. He knew the easiest choice for me was to reject Nancy, especially as she was not there to argue her case. Why should I replace the idealized mother of my imagination with the common slut he had depicted? For years I had daily looked at the features of the beautiful woman I had come to believe was my mother. Agnes's portrait dominated not only my bedroom but also my mind. Hers was the last face I saw each night before I closed my eyes in sleep and I woke to her innocent gaze each morning. I felt I knew her because of my dealings with her sister, Rose Maylie, and, rightly or wrongly, I assumed that all Rose's virtues belonged equally to Agnes.

The story of Agnes Fleming as I had been told it was indeed a tragic one. She was the elder daughter of a retired naval officer who, at the age of nineteen, had the misfortune to fall in love with a rich and handsome man named Edwin Leeford. Mr Brownlow informed me that he was a very fine character and I trust his judgement. He knew Edwin Leeford very well because he had been engaged to Edwin's sister until her untimely early death. Maybe some of his passion for his lost love explains why Mr Brownlow also loved Edwin, whom he came to regard as his best friend. According to him, Edwin's family had forced him when he was still a youth into an extremely unhappy arranged marriage with an older and hard-hearted woman. The two had nothing in common and she was as wicked as Edwin was good. Even the birth of a son, whom they christened Edward, failed to end the anguish of their ill-assorted union. Indifference inevitably gave place to dislike and dislike to hatred and hatred to loathing. As time passed cold formalities were replaced by open conflict and eventual separation. Thus Edwin Leeford was still just in his early thirties and yet had been apart from his wife and son for over a decade when he met Agnes and fell passionately in love with her.

Mr Brownlow stated that the union of

Edwin and Agnes was formed in heaven but Edwin's earlier dismal marriage meant it was nevertheless condemned to hell. Edwin refused to risk bigamy and merely told Agnes there was a secret family reason why he could not marry her in public. She, trusting him too deeply, surrendered herself as if they were married, losing what none could ever give her back. And I was the bastard product of their illicit but undoubtedly heartfelt love. For business reasons my father had to leave England for Rome before he could set in place appropriate arrangements to cover up her shame. And whilst in that city he contracted a fatal illness. Though long estranged, his first wife made sure she was at his deathbed and thus gained access to his final correspondence. This comprised a will and a letter to my mother in which he told her of his love and what he had intended to do for her had he lived. The will left only small annuities to his wife and legitimate son. The bulk of his estate was left to Agnes and her child, should it survive. I was therefore effectively Edwin Leeford's sole heir.

Needless to say, Edwin's embittered wife destroyed both the letter and the will, hoping that there was no copy of the latter somewhere else. She thus ensured that his entire property fell to her and her son,

Edward Leeford. Meanwhile Agnes's father removed my unfortunate mother to a remote corner of Wales, where her shame could be well hidden. Who knows what passed between them in their isolation, but there must have been very harsh and bitter words because Agnes eventually chose to flee from her unhappy home. The result was tragic. With nowhere to go, Agnes ended up a homeless wanderer until she was tragically found lying in a street with her clothes sodden and her shoes worn to pieces. She was taken to the nearest workhouse and there she died giving birth to me. Charles Dickens in his account has the exhausted Agnes imperfectly articulate the words, 'Let me see the child, and die', but that was probably just his literary licence.

My grandfather was distraught at her disappearance, and shortly afterwards he died of a broken heart, not knowing either the fate of his daughter or his grandchild. I thus grew up in the cruel poverty of the workhouse. In contrast my half-brother Edward Leeford reached his manhood surrounded by all the things money could buy and all purchased with the wealth of my inheritance. However, at one level his life was not any happier than mine. At least I was a child born in love whereas Edward Leeford was a child conceived in hate. Certainly Mr Brownlow was quick to inform me that Edward's upbringing had created a very seriously flawed man. He used to joke sometimes that if I was known as Oliver Twist, then my stepbrother should have been renamed 'Edward Twisted'. There is no doubt that his profligate and debauched lifestyle soon destroyed not only much of his fortune but also his looks and his reputation.

Edward was eventually forced to flee London society to avoid arrest for a series of crimes. He retired to some family estates in the West Indies, his face and mind scarred by the pox. When he returned to England, he did so to fulfil the dying wishes of his mother. She had made him promise to seek out Agnes Fleming and any child she might have produced because she was fearful that at some stage, if another version of Edwin Leeford's will was discovered, they might challenge him for the return of what was rightly theirs. Assuming the name of Monks lest the police capture him for his earlier misdeeds, Edward's enquiries eventually led him to the workhouse where my mother had died. They also led to his pursuit of me. It was his malicious wish to ensure that I should live as miserable a life as possible. Imagine therefore his delight to discover that one of his former associates, Fagin, actually knew of my whereabouts. And imagine his subsequent frustration at my escape, first to the home of his hated father's best friend, Mr Brownlow, and then to the home of Mrs Maylie, who was the benefactress who had taken in my mother's younger sister, Rose. She had saved her from destitution at the time of her father's untimely death, following the disappearance of her sister.

As I have already indicated, I believed it was Nancy who had thwarted both Monks' and Fagin's endeavours to destroy me. Although Dickens viewed her as not just a whore but also a murderess, I found this difficult to reconcile with my memories of Nancy's kindness to me and to other unfortunates. I had no wish to replace Agnes Fleming with such a woman as a mother and yet I had to know the truth. Was my likeness to Agnes Fleming only in the mind of Mr Brownlow, who had never actually met her and whose picture of her was based only on a portrait that was perhaps not even a good likeness? Was Edward Leeford equally mistaken in thinking I was his stepbrother? Was Nancy's interest in me really kindled by the fact I was her son? And, if so, who might be my father? How and why had Mr Brownlow acquired greater wealth to bequeath to me? And what had happened to Agnes Fleming's true son? These and many more questions so obsessed me that I knew I could not leave the matter alone.

Although Dickens had assumed that our conversation would end the matter, he had unwittingly given me the vehicle for more research. Before I had left his house, he had given me one vital piece of information. It was the whereabouts of Betsy, Nancy's closest friend. To my surprise, Dickens had not only kept in touch with Betsy but also secured her placement as the controller of a home for fallen women that he had helped to set up. It was capable of holding thirteen inmates at a time and he told me that Betsy was one of the two superintendents who ran it. I recognized that she, more than anyone else, might know if there were any truth behind Fagin's accusations, and I wrote requesting a meeting with her. Having received a gracious and affirmative reply, I made my way to see Betsy, without informing Dickens of my intentions.

The house for fallen women was aptly called Redemption Cottage and was near Shepherd's Bush. It was an unprepossessing building from the outside, austere and forbidding. It had the air of a house that had known more prosperous days but was entering into a slow and inexorable decline. Its mortar was crumbling and its paintwork, such as remained, peeling. Only the well-tended garden sang a welcome. It was full of flowers, a festive mix of yellows, blues, purples, and reds, which even the soot-laden fog of London could not hide. A sallow-faced, red-haired, rather sulky young woman answered my knock at the door. After surveying me from head to toe through its glass panel, she applied a large key to the lock and gave me entry. I told her my name and that I was expected and, after a moment's hesitation in which she studied my face with a strange intensity, she led me into the parlour.

The woman who greeted me when I entered was very different from the Betsy I remembered. Then she had been a scarlet-dressed girl with blue sparkling eyes and brown wavy hair for whom men had been prepared to pay handsomely. Now she was a smartly dressed woman in a well-preserved black silk gown and a handsome white shawl, a mature woman with greying hair and a nose that appeared more hook-shaped than I remembered. Then she had been the laughing, semi-drunk companion, always in Nancy's shadow. Now she appeared imposingly tall and the strength of her character was evident in her shrewd eyes, which were deep-sunken above cheekbones that jutted squarely across her face. Her gaze seemed to enter into my very head and to search my innermost thoughts and desires. Despite the unhappy memories my appearance must have evoked, she gave me a kindly welcome and smilingly enquired whether I minded her calling me 'Master Oliver' in memory of former times. I readily assented.

'Before we speak of the matters that have brought you here,' she said, 'let me show you the work we do.'

For the next half-hour or so she took a pride in guiding me around her domain. Some say that a person cannot change from their evil ways but Betsy was truly a woman transformed by the Christian faith she had embraced. No longer was she the dirty, slip-shod and dishevelled person I had known in Fagin's den. Instead she was an angel of mercy. Her passionate and moving concern for the welfare of the home's inmates was so heartfelt that it soon became immediately obvious. I can still recall much of what she told me and I think it bears repeating, though much of it is irrelevant to my tale. Amid the horrors I depict in these pages, it is good to give space to dwell at least for a time on acts of Christian charity. These were Betsy's words as I recall them:

'Master Oliver, I have found deep contentment and happiness here. I say nothing but the truth when I tell you that this house enables some extremely unhappy women to become a blessing to themselves and others instead of being just a curse on society. Misfortune and distress are the only introduction that a woman requires to enter our walls. Here you will find former shoplifters and pickpockets, domestic servants who have been seduced by their masters, girls who have attempted suicide, and whores who have escaped their pimps. We have poor girls from ragged schools, destitute girls who have applied at police stations for aid, starving needlewomen who have been unable to pay the rent on their furnished lodgings without resorting to prostitution, and violent girls committed to prison for disturbances in ill-conducted workhouses. Most of those we help are in their early twenties but, disgrace that it is, we have taken some as young as seven or eight years old. Nearly all are ignorant. What almost all share in common is that they have had little or no experience of kindness in their lives. I don't need to tell you how lonely and isolated that makes you feel.

'When a girl arrives we ask her to tell us her history and we record it in a book. Believe me, if ever it were to be published, this book would be such a damning indictment of our society that England's reputation would be forever blighted. But once their history is known we rarely talk further about it because we encourage them to look to a better future. Our aim, Master Oliver, is to offer these young women, who have lost their character and lapsed into sin, a sense of hope and a chance to start their lives anew in Australia or America or elsewhere. We are not naïve. We have no extravagant expectations. It is not always easy to persuade a girl to work for many hours a day in order to earn what she can gain in a few minutes by simply opening her legs. We have faced many failures and disappointments but I consider this enterprise well rewarded if but a third of those we receive are saved and fly from crime and prostitution. Does not Heaven itself rejoice over one sinner who repents?'

I nodded my assent and Betsy, grateful for my approval (for not all of society would agree with this sentiment), warmly grasped my hands between hers before continuing her account.

'I have learnt that the past is something to be largely forgotten, Master Oliver, and that what we do now and in the future is far more important. The fact that we offer the girls forgiveness does not make us soft. On the contrary, we impose a strict routine and expect the girls to be practical and active. They get up at six in the morning, winter and summer, and we hold prayers and a scripture reading before breakfast. The day is then partly taken up with housework undertaken on a rota. Two work in the bedrooms, two in the general living room, two in the kitchens, two in the scullery, and five in the laundry. They make and mend their own clothes, although we never allow them to keep any spare clothes under their control lest they attempt to sneak out and sell them. Indeed we keep all their clothes under lock and key in a wardrobe room. The rest of the day is taken up with two hours of lessons in the mornings and a few hours in the afternoons when the girls do needlework or are helped to write letters to relatives or someone who has been kind to them (if such exist). Those who can read do so out loud for the benefit of the rest.

'All our meals are communal. Dinner is at one and tea at six. After tea the girls are allowed a half-hour in the garden if the weather permits. Three times a fortnight a local clergyman joins us in the evenings and provides additional religious instruction. He's a good man because there are some clergy who will have nothing to do with this place. How they square that with following our Lord and Master I do not know! Every evening we hold evening prayers half an hour before bedtime at nine. They say temptation does not knock on the door, it leans on the doorbell, and so we have to be constantly vigilant. For that reason no one has a room to herself and we place those we can trust most as the bedmates of those we can trust least. Nobody makes her own bed so they cannot contemplate hiding things and all cupboards in the house are kept locked and the keys are never left lying about. We even keep the garden gate locked at night, so they cannot just wander out.'

'It sounds rather prison-like to me, Betsy,' I interrupted. 'Why should these poor unfortunates change their way of life if they are given no opportunity to show their better qualities?'

'Oh, but they are, Master Oliver. We know reducing temptation is not enough to change lives. Hence we also seek to reward good behaviour. Marks are given for truthfulness, industry, good temper, punctuality, cleanliness, propriety of conduct and conversation, and a sedate and patient manner. A girl can earn up to thirty-six good marks a day and each girl is promised she will receive when she leaves six shillings and sixpence for every thousand marks she has earned. Any girl behaving badly in any of the categories can expect to lose forty marks, but it is encouragement rather than threats that are the key to our successes. If we see a girl wavering, we remind her how much she has changed and what great hopes we have for her. We beg her not to throw away her chance of transforming her life for the better. We also encourage mutual support and care for those outside the community. For example, any leftovers from our meals are made into soup for the sick and the poor.

'Our Lord can give the strength required to change one's life. I know that from personal experience, Master Oliver. Without the presence of Jesus in my heart, I do not believe my life would be as it now is. Prayer is a constant and necessary feature of our life here and our prayers do not go unanswered.

'The average stay required to give a girl the ability to start her life afresh is about a year, although a few have remained longer because they were slower to learn their reading. We then arrange for three or four at a time to go to America or Australia so that they can make a completely new start away from any of their former connections, which might draw them back into their previous lives. Each girl is given a letter of recommendation and placed under the charge of a respectable family of emigrants as a nurse or servant. We try to keep in touch with them and some take the trouble to write and let us know how they are getting on. Here, let me show you a recent letter.'

We re-entered her room and Betsy fumbled through some papers that lay on her desk. She passed on to me a carefully folded note, saying I was welcome to keep it because she had already replied to it. It was written in a rough but perfectly readable hand. As I read its contents, she sat upright in her seat, hands clasped in her lap, and I sensed she was judging me by my response to its humble contents. She need not have worried — I was moved by its simplicity and heartfelt gratitude. I still have the original in my possession and I treasure its plain honesty far more than the most beautifully phrased passage of any novel by Dickens or Trollope. This is what the letter said and I make no apology for its lack of grammar, inaccurate punctuation and faulty spelling:

My Honnoured Lady,
I have taken the liberty of writing to you again to let you know how I am going on since I last wrote Home — for you did indeed giv a home to one who had none. I cannot describe my feelings when I received your most kind letter, I first read my letter then I cried but it was with tears of joy. You will be plesed to no that my new

Husband is very kind to me and we live very happy and comfortable together we have a nice garden where we grow all we want we have sown some peas and turnips and I helped to do some we have three such nice fat pigs and we killed one last week he was so fat that he could not see out of his eyes he used to have to sit down to eat. My two little birds are gone — one dide and the other flew away but I have got such a sweet cat. My Husband was going out one day and heard her crying and he fetched her in she was so thin. He tells that if we do well then one day he mite take me back to see you if we live so long, but I think he is only making game of me. My Honnoured Lady I can never feel grateful enough for you kindness to me and wot you did for me at my happy Home, I often wish I could come and see you again once more and all my kind friends which I hope I may one day please God.

Betsy watched me as I read its simple message of gratitude, and then said, 'Keep it, Master Oliver, and let it remind you of what this place achieves, because its writer had a terrible history when she came to us at the age of sixteen. She had got herself into trouble for making a disturbance at the workhouse gate when refused relief. She had been a professed tramp for six or seven years, knew of no relation, and had had no friends but one old woman, whose very name she appeared to be uncertain about. She was dressed only in rags, had no shoes for her feet, and had seldom slept in a bed. She told us her father, a scaffold builder, had 'lost' her on London Bridge when she was nine or ten years old. I suspect he probably purposely abandoned her, although she refused to believe that. Not that she was naïve. Far from it. She was old beyond her years because poverty and starvation had forced her to grant the most despicable sexual favours to the dross of the London streets.

'If you regard any of the work I do with favour, then please remember that I am simply repaying some of the kindness shown to me by Nancy. You have to seize what friendship you can find and that's exactly what Nancy and me did. I still think of her each day and wish she could be here to help my girls and me. Believe me, she helped me as much as she assisted you. I know Mr Dickens has a most unfortunate view of her character and he may not have been very kind in what he told you about her. However, I would like her to be remembered for her many virtues and not her few vices. You know

113

she was far from perfect, especially if she had had too much to drink, and I know Nancy committed many sins in her life. But I do not wish to be the one to throw any stone against her, because I know she was also much sinned against. As indeed was I in my youth. The world is not a fair place, Master Oliver, as you yourself know.'

I indicated my assent and urged her to now tell me what she could about herself and Nancy. Sensing that I would brook no further delay, Betsy acknowledged that the time had come for her to tell me the little she knew. It turned out to be more than I was expecting.

7

Betsy's Story

'My own story is not an edifying one but let me begin with it because, Master Oliver, I sense that you do not view me as unworthy. Recounting my past shame may help you discover more about Nancy and why she meant so much to so many of us. I came up from the countryside when I was still a girl, not above fifteen, in order to live with an elderly aunt of mine. My mother had died in giving birth to me and my father had tired of having me. He was a farmer near Bath, but only in a small way. I was very pleased to be in London, and liked sneaking out of my aunt's house when I had the opportunity of doing so unnoticed.

'One night I met a handsome-looking man who chatted with me in a flattering way. I, like the innocent I was, answered him unsuspectingly, and he asked me if I had long been in London. Not thinking, I told him all about myself. He went away saying he was very glad to have made my acquaintance. He told me if I would say nothing about our meeting to my aunt, he would see me about the same time the next night and take me out for the evening. I was entirely taken in by his good looks and the next evening, I am ashamed to say, I met him as he appointed, and two or three times thereafter.

'One night we walked further than usual until I pressed him to return, fearing my aunt would find us out. However, he said he was not feeling well and he asked me to stay with him just a little longer. He wanted me to wait while he took a short rest in a nearby house, which belonged to an old woman who was a friend of his. He reassured me that, if I were concerned about further delay, he would put me in a cab. Worried about him, for I did not know what had caused his illness, I agreed to accompany him. We found the door to his friend's house half-open when we arrived at the house. We entered and walked into a well-lit room, full of gaudily dressed and brazenly painted young women. My friend greeted an old grey-haired lady who was talking to several of them. She told me they were her daughters. This made my gentleman laugh and she fiercely ordered them out of the room.

'I didn't like the feel of the place, and I asked to be sent home. My gentleman friend said he would order a cab but I must have a drink while I waited for its arrival. I foolishly assented. No sooner had I drunk some wine than I felt very sleepy, so sleepy that they advised me to rest a little and promised to send a messenger to my aunt to allay any anxiety she might have at my failure to return home. Of course, Master Oliver, I had been drugged. In my semi-conscious state I was systematically raped, not only by the man who had so basely deceived me, but also by his associates, who came to join in his fun. Eventually I passed out and did not wake till the next morning.

'I was horrified by the extent of my ruin. It was even worse when I discovered from the old grey-haired woman that the man responsible had seen my deflowering as a cure for his suspected venereal disease. For some days I was inconsolable, and cried like a child to be killed or sent back to my aunt. The woman made me sign papers that I could not read. She told me the papers placed me entirely in her power and I must do as I was told. You can imagine the rest. Each night she sent different men to my bed. I never knew how much or how little each customer had paid, only what acts were expected of me and for how long. If I resisted, I was beaten. My whore-keeper's one act of self-interested compassion was to provide me with a witches' brew of alum and sulphate of zinc with which to wash away what otherwise might lead to pregnancy.

'This life of slavery went on for some months before I managed to escape. By then I knew that my aunt would have nothing to do with me. I would be soiled beyond redemption in her eyes. And so I escaped one tyranny for another. The rat-infested streets became my home and I was more susceptible to assault there than I had been in the whorehouse. I slept on doorsteps and tried to earn a living by collecting old bones and dog turds for a tannery, but soon I was so reduced by hunger that I allowed myself to be used again by whoever would have me. Some tricked me, taking their pleasure without payment. If I obtained the money to go into a cheap lodging it made little difference to my safety. We lay all packed together on a full night, a dozen boys and girls squeezed into one bed, some at the foot and some at the top, and, in the hot stifling atmosphere, sometimes entirely naked. Most of us got half-drunk if we could afford it. If we didn't, the bed was wasted because the bugs and the bad air prevented us from sleeping properly. I won't go into particulars, but whatever could take place in acts between boys and girls usually did. We knew no better.

'It was Nancy who came to my rescue. She found me curled up in a heap outside a wretched tumbledown hovel in a stinking alleyway, which swarmed with untended infants. She took me back to her brothel. Although Fagin was a miserly pimp, Nancy knew he would at least provide me with a proper roof over my head, some more acceptable clothing and decent meals to eat. It seems strange now but I was so grateful to him for taking me in. I gave myself to whatever men he directed as if I was serving my saviour. It used to amuse Nancy. Her view of Fagin was rightly far more critical. She knew he never acted out of genuine kindness to anyone and, as far as he was concerned, I was just one more way of adding to his income. In contrast to him, although she could be a devil when she chose, Nancy was prone to moments of pure philanthropy, offering help to those in need even when she had little herself. I loved her, Master Oliver, because she was what I had long lacked. She was my first genuine friend.'

Betsy could not help shedding a tear as she recalled this and I stretched out my hands to hers, grasping them to acknowledge I understood her feelings. She took a few moments to compose herself and then resumed.

'We frequently drank ourselves stupid because in that way we could forget at least for a time what our life was like in the black, stinking, shelterless alleys in which we plied our trade. Sometimes the gin led Nancy to speak about her past and gradually I learnt her history. It was just as unfortunate as mine, but her troubles had begun at a far earlier age. Nancy grew up in one of this city's many slum districts. I know it well and a stinking permanent fog overhangs the entire neighbourhood. Most of the men who live there, if not professional criminals, are of that dangerous class which exists between pauper and convict. Most of the women carry on some miserable domestic craft for little reward. Some weave cages and baskets from cane. Some make matchboxes, clothes pegs, flypapers, and the like. Others take in stitchwork or washing or engage in selling the pelts of strayed and stolen cats. Untended infants relieve themselves on stairs and passageways, whilst their older brothers and sisters go out to scavenge and pilfer what they can from the streets. Some of the prematurely old children attend the twice-weekly hiring mart where they can offer themselves to unsavory employers. Some of the better-off families supplement their income by keeping pigs and cows, feeding them on the refuse that clutters the streets, but this adds to the unhealthy environment because often the animals are tubercular.

'Growing up in such an environment, Nancy learnt the hard way that seizing opportunities and having no scruples was the key to survival. From childhood she was taught to walk the streets, regardless of the weather or temperature, begging and picking up anything she thought might be edible or saleable. Sometimes she was given a roll of matches with strict instructions not to return home until she had sold them. If she tried to return before the task was fulfilled, she was severely beaten. For a time she was also taken into the workhouse but only faced fresh cruelties there.

'Then suddenly she experienced a different world. A church mission rescued her at the age of six or seven from the hellhole that was her life. They taught her to read and write and to look to Jesus. Unfortunately for her, they then handed her over to be maidservant to an elderly couple. It was not long before, like many a servant girl, she found her employer began demanding sexual gratification from her. One day he repeatedly hit her with his cane when she resisted. She threatened to inform his wife and he threw her out on the street.

'She was still just ten years old, Master Oliver. Like mine, her lifestyle became one of sleeping where she could, eating whatever she could get, and surviving either by begging, stealing, or selling her body. It was one of Fagin's lads who saw that she had potential beyond the average whore and took her to The Three Cripples, where she was easily persuaded to join the gang.

'At first Fagin used her talents primarily to earn money for him as a prostitute, but, like all his workers, he trained her in the finer arts of stealing. She quickly understood that the more energy she devoted to stealing the less she had to sell herself. She became adept at hiding in her clothes the property stolen by the boys and thus masking their crimes. She was not averse to luring small well-clothed children into some deserted alleyway where they could be skinned of their boots and clothes. Sometimes she would pick up some tipsy man and take him to a secluded spot where some of Fagin's lads were waiting to rob him. Shoplifting seemed to come naturally to her. But if thieving was more congenial and more rewarding, it did not prevent Fagin demanding she use her body when it suited his needs. Many a servant has given away his master's secrets in Nancy's arms and thus opened the door to a piece of profitable housebreaking. It was, of course, through this trade that she eventually met Bill Sikes.

'I never understood what she saw in him. You know what he was like, with his scowling eyes, thunderous brows, and frequently unshaven face. Even when he was sober, his temper was foul, but, with the drink in him, he was often like the devil himself. Many the time I've seen him pulverize another man's face with his fists for some imagined slight. His so-called friends feared him more than they liked him, but they respected his housebreaking abilities. When sober, Bill was a formidable thief, quick to assess the weakness of a property and quicker still to sniff out where its most valuable contents lay hidden. Fagin loathed him but valued his services too much to do without them. Normally Bill preferred doing his business with Fagin when no one was around because he was paranoiac about being squealed upon. As a consequence his first meeting with Nancy was a much-delayed one, considering she had been in the Jew's service since she was a child. But once their paths crossed he was as passionately drawn to her as she was to him.

'For the first time Bill had found a woman who was prepared to stand up to him.

Although he was quick to beat her for any opposition she expressed, he secretly admired it. And Nancy was intensely loyal to Bill. She said that she had let him fill the place that had been a blank through all her wretched life. Fagin's talk of her betraying him would have appeared nonsense to all of us who knew her, but for her behaviour over you. Bill may have been a brute but he was not a stupid man. Even he could sense that your arrival powerfully changed Nancy and that her relationship with you was even more significant to her than her love for him. Hence his animosity towards you. Normally Fagin's lads were below his gaze and beneath his interest. He started to beat her in a way that was cruelly vindictive and which all of us resented, except her. She appeared to recognize that the cause of his brutality was his jealousy and that his jealousy spoke of his deep love for her. And Nancy, you have to remember, had never been loved by a man. Only used by many men. For a whore to know she is genuinely loved is a rare experience. I never heard her complain of the way he hit her and she, poor soul, would always endeavour to hide the bruises as best she could.

'One evening I came across Nancy after a particularly vicious attack. I pleaded with her to end Bill's jealousy by making clear she had no further interest in you. It was then, Master Oliver, that at last she finally told me her secret. She informed me that you were her long-lost son. It came as a shock to me, although I had long known that Nancy had once given birth. The stretch marks on her body bore witness to that. Indeed, she used to joke sometimes about how stupid many of her customers were because, despite these indicators, she could still persuade them she was a virgin. Virginity was an obscene joke as far as Nancy was concerned. The money charged for supposed 'virgins' and 'fresh country girls' was always far higher for the heavy-spending debauchees who frequented many of the whorehouses. She laughed at the so-called 'dolly-mops', who gave of their real virginity to a spruce young medical student or junior clerk without realizing its market value. Occasionally she would enjoy seducing some youth into his first experience of sex, and then, having taken his money, would tell him how inept he was or whisper into his ear that he ought to know she had syphilis. A cruel joke but I cannot blame her. Nancy and I both knew it was likely that disease would eventually catch us both.

'Nancy told me that when she was still little more than a child herself she had failed to take the necessary precautions. By the time Fagin became aware of her condition it was too late for an abortion. She gave birth to a son only to have him promptly removed from her arms. Fagin told her he was handed over as an orphan to a workhouse but he refused to tell her which one. All she could remember of the child she held so briefly in her arms was a small birthmark on its back. When she saw you semi-naked and saw that very same mark on your skin, Master Oliver, she was convinced that you were her lost child. From that moment on she determined to prevent you facing the life she had had. I cannot tell you whether you are indeed her child, for she may have been mistaken, but this I can tell you. It brought out in her all the qualities that her way of life had for so long largely suppressed. Nancy loved you as only a mother can love. It drove her to seek your safety above her own. As you are all too painfully aware, it cost Nancy her life.'

'Enough, enough, Betsy, enough,' I cried. 'Please do not make me feel even guiltier than I do. I never wished for Bill to murder her.'

Betsy drew breath as if judging whether to say more and then, deciding to do so, she dropped her astounding news to my disconcerted mind:

'I'm not convinced that Bill did murder

her, Master Oliver. Nancy told me something else, something I have never before revealed to anyone. But, if you are her son, you need to know. Nancy informed me that someone else was threatening her life. She told me there had been two attempts to poison those closest to her and she believed she might be the next victim. I am sure you remember how for a time illness reduced Sikes almost to a corpse. Despite his strong constitution he became as weak as water and was reduced to such a parlous state that it was only Nancy's constant care that enabled him to survive. She nursed him day and night to the point of exhaustion. Afterwards she told me she was certain that it was not a disease which had caused his suffering but poison. Rose Maylie was taken seriously ill at about the same time. You will be aware of how precious close she came to dying, although in her case it was a doctor's skill that nursed her back to health. Nancy was sure her illness was the work of the same person and she was terrified that the poisoner might strike her down next, thus preventing her from continuing to look after your welfare. However, she had no idea who was seeking to destroy her and those to whom she was close.

'For that reason I have sometimes thought it is possible, Master Oliver that her death was not at the hands of Bill. When I found her poor body, her head beaten beyond recognition, I could not believe Bill could have done that much damage to her, brute though he was. Could a man who loved her so much really destroy her beauty so savagely and totally? Or did the unknown poisoner she feared turn to a more violent method of disposing of her and then make Bill appear to be the murderer? Unfortunately, I remember little of what happened after the discovery of her body because I became hysterical. I screamed and raved and even beat my head on the walls. In the end they put me into a straitjacket and took me to hospital. By the time I was released the entire circle in which we lived for so long had been destroyed in the wake of her murder. I have mourned her loss as only a true friend can, but I suspect the truth of what happened to Nancy will never now be known.'

Needless to say, Betsy's account moved me greatly, especially her references to the poisoning of Bill Sikes and Rose Maylie. Although I felt it inappropriate to tell her anything of Dickens's story, it seemed to me blindingly obvious that Mary Hogarth had been a third victim of the unknown poisoner and, if so, Dickens was sadly mistaken in his view of Nancy's guilt. However, the identity of such a poisoner was a total mystery. I told Betsy it was essential that I should talk to others of Fagin's gang because one of them might have some clues to his or her identity. Betsy hesitated, and then replied that there was only one whom she still saw occasionally. This was Tommy Chitling. She smiled and I knew why. In the old days the Dodger and Charley Bates had teased Chitling horribly about his affection for Betsy. I suspected that he was still attracted to her and that she enjoyed his attentions, even though she had sworn never to marry any man. Betsy's blush confirmed my suspicions. I thanked her for all of her honesty and, despite her protestations, insisted on donating some money for her charity work. I told her it was my way of thanking Nancy for rescuing me. And it was.

8

Ratcatching

As I approached The Three Cripples, or rather The Cripples as it was more commonly known, it looked very little different from the outside from how it had appeared when I was a child, although it was much smaller than I remembered. When all those years ago I had been dragged inside by Bill Sikes, I had found it a very intimidating place because it was filled with a numerous company drawn from the worst gutters of London. The men seemed invariably coarse and vulgar. Most had consumed far too much alcohol to control their passions. The women, who were its main attraction, ranged from mere girls who had not yet learnt to hide their fear and aversion to the tasks they were expected to fulfil, to older women who had painted their harsh faces in a futile attempt to disguise the ravages of their soulless lifestyle. I had hoped never to enter its filthy walls again, but my quest now gave me no option.

When I entered it the place was so full of dense tobacco smoke that at first I could scarce see anything. By degrees, however, my eyes became accustomed to the murk and I saw that its clientele had changed but little. I recognized the man behind the bar as Tommy Chitling, though if he had passed me in the street I would not have done so. He had grown much more corpulent than when I had known him and a life spent largely indoors had rendered his features grey and pallid. Whatever Betsy saw in him, it was evidently not his looks or his dress. His hair was greasy and unwashed, his skin was pockmarked and scarred, his mouth was marred by some of the most blackened and decayed teeth I had ever seen, and his nose was misshapen, probably as a result of some drunken brawl. His appearance was not helped by the dirt-encrusted clothes he wore or by the cut of his small beard, which seemed to give his features a rather ratlike look. And the smell of vermin seemed to permeate the atmosphere around him. The reason for this soon became clear. When he had become the landlord of The Three Cripples, he had altered the entertainment it offered by converting it into an establishment that entertained its customers by holding organized rat-fights.

The front of the long bar was crowded with men smoking and drinking. Most were talking about dogs and some had brought their fierce animals with them. These were struggling in their masters' arms, whining and barking. Nearly all of them were marked with nasty scars from vicious bites inflicted by the rats they were trained to fight. The walls were adorned with sporting pictures and brass decorated dog-collars made of leather. On special display was a black one with a silver clasp, which, I subsequently learnt, was to be the prize in a rat-match the following week. Over the fireplace was a square glazed box in which was displayed a stuffed former prize-winning bulldog with its glass eyes protruding as if the poor creature had been deeply shocked by its extinction. Its unblinking gaze stared out at the rat pit itself.

If you have never seen one, a rat pit resembles a small circus, some six feet in diameter. It is surrounded by a wall with a high wooden rim that reaches to elbow level. The branches of a gas lamp are arranged to hang over the pit to illuminate its white-painted floor. A few moments after my entrance most of the audience began clambering upon tables and benches to view the entertainment, and a few of the more daring even began hanging over the side of the pit itself in their determination to get the best possible sight of the forthcoming action. For the wealthier a private box provided a particularly good vantage point and it was into this that I was directed by Tommy Chitling, once he had espied me and welcomed me. I thus found myself an unwilling participant in the savage show that was about to commence.

A rusty wire cage, filled with a dark, moving mass of large and evil-looking rats, was brought in and the excited barking from the dogs became almost unbearable. Tommy made the round of the room, handling each dog in turn, feeling and squeezing its legs and paws and scrutinizing its eyes. The first dog was chosen. Despite its small size, it was a fearsome-looking brute. One of Tommy Chitling's men then began pulling the rats out of the cage by their tails and jerking them into the arena. He counted out a dozen. Bets were exchanged all around the room before the selected terrier was thrown into the pit. Immediately it advanced on the trapped rats. Some sprang up at his face, making him momentarily draw back and bark his defiance. Then the dog resumed his attack, snatching a rat in his mouth. It curled around and fastened its yellow teeth on his neck before the life was crushed out of it. The dog seized another, shaking it furiously and bashing its head on the floor repeatedly. This made the crowd roar with laughter. I closed my eyes to avoid seeing more but my imagination filled the gap till silence indicated that all the rats were dead.

However, this was only a taster. The blood-flecked terrier was removed, its mouth rinsed with peppermint and water, and once again rats were dropped one by one into the pit. This time I reckon forty were released. They gathered together into a heaving black mass that reached one-third up the arena's side. They were all rats caught in the sewers and the stink that rose up from them was like that of an open drain. The man who had thrown them into the pit amused himself by flicking at them with a large handkerchief and offering them the lighted end of his cigar. Some of the creatures sniffed at the latter and then rapidly retreated as their noses were singed. A bull terrier, nearly mad with excitement and struggling to get loose, was allowed to jump into the pit once bets had been taken as to how many rats the dog could kill in eight minutes.

A stopwatch was started. The moment the dog was free, he became quiet in a most businesslike manner and then rushed at the rats. In a short time a dozen rats were lying bleeding on the pit's white floor so it was streaked with rodent blood. One rat managed to attach itself to the bull terrier's snout but the dog dashed its head against the wall of the arena, leaving a patch of blood as if a large and overripe fruit had been crushed there.

When the eight minutes were up the owner of the dog caught hold of its collar and held it whilst its many victims were counted. The dog panted and stretched out its head in a vain attempt to see the remaining rats. The poor little creatures seemed to forget their danger and commenced crawling about or cleaning themselves with a strange nibbling action. A few advanced, sniffing, to within a few paces of their former enemy. To the anger and frustration of its owner, the count showed the dog had not killed enough to warrant a second go. It was removed and a plentiful supply of halfpence was thrown by the onlookers into the pit to signal they wanted more. Tommy Chitling invited the crowd to fill up their glasses before the next dog was given its turn. But I had had more than enough of the event and begged him to take me to his private quarters. He seemed amused by my squeamishness but did as I asked.

His sitting room was illuminated by a couple of gas lights and their glare revealed a number of cages filled with yet more vermin. But these were Tommy's tame pets. To my dismay, he insisted on showing me some of his more curious specimens, but I felt I had no option but to humour him if I was to get any information. Some were piebald and others white, with pink unwholesome eyes. He took a few out to show me and handled them without the least fear. The poor creatures made no attempt to bite him, appearing to have lost any notion of regaining their liberty. In one of the cages he had a couple of entirely white rats confined together, and, pointing at them, he remarked, 'Old English rats are normally jet-black so I'm hoping they'll breed and then, when I have enough, I can introduce them into the show as a speciality.'

Tommy was clearly upset when I failed to hide my intense dislike for his pets. Clutching my arm, he muttered in my ear, 'Don't think badly of me, Mr Twist, for these rat shows. Better animals suffer than women. And believe me, sir, I am a real benefactor to this city because not only do I reduce the number of vermin but I pay for the privilege.'

'What do you mean?' I asked.

'Well, sir, I have a number of very poor families depending on me. They supply me with rats. I have to say that they are the most ignorant people I ever come near. They can scarce speak properly so that I have difficulty sometimes understanding what they say. When the harvest is got in and they can earn a living in no other way, they go hunting for rats and I give a halfpenny each for them. Often the rats brought to me are caught in warehouses because that way the ketchers get paid twice if they're lucky. Once by me and once by them that owns the warehouses. I should think I buy from three hundred to seven hundred rats a week, but I've had as many as a thousand in this house at one time. They'll consume a large sack of barley-meal a week and, if you don't give them good grub, they will eat one another.

'Don't look down on me. My occupation demands its own skills. I can tell a barn rat from a ship rat or a sewer rat in a minute, and I have to separate my stock when I buy them or they'd fight to the death. There's six or seven types of rat, and if we don't sort 'em they tear one another to pieces. It's dangerous work for the handlers, Mr Twist. The bite of sewer or water-ditch rats is very bad, as they live off filth. I've been near dead three times from bites. When a rat's bite touches the bone, it makes you feel faint and it bleeds dreadful, just as if you had been stuck with a knife. I once had the teeth of a rat break in my finger and putrify till I had the broken bits pulled out. Get a bad bite and you know all about it. It festers and forms a hard throbbing sore that never properly heals. You can see my hands is all covered with scars from rat bites and I'm also marked elsewhere. In fact over the years I've been bitten nearly everywhere, even where I can't name to you, sir.'

I looked at his damaged hands and winced. He brushed aside my tentative expressions of sympathy and began to speak of the matter I had really come to see him about. Betsy had told him of my purpose and he had agreed to tell me all he knew. This did not stop him telling me he spoke only with reluctance.

'I only agreed to see you to please her and not for any delight in us meeting again. The past is the past as far as I am concerned and I'd rather forget those days. However, if speak I must I'll tell you more than I've ivver told anyone else, even Betsy, provided you promise not to tell her. She's so fond of Nancy there'd be no holding her back if she knew.'

'I promise you that I will not tell Betsy what you say,' I replied, loathe to lose any chance of hearing something of importance from him.

'They say rats will leave a sinking ship, Mr Twist. Well, that's what happened when the news of Nancy's murder broke and that blackguard Fagin was seized. Charley and I made our lucky escape up the wash'us chimney but a new lad we called Bolter failed to live up to his assumed name. He was caught trying to hide in an empty water butt, stupid fool that he was.'

'Ay,' I interrupted, 'That does not surprise me.' Bolter's real name was Noah Claypole and I had very strong reason to dislike him for the way he had maltreated me when I worked for the undertaker, Mr Sowerberry.

'We all knew feeling was running very high', continued Chitling. 'As you know, Nancy had been a popular gal in the neighbourhood and it was known the Jew had had a hand in her death. No one liked Fagin and it was no surprise that the police had to rescue him from being torn apart by the mob. Bruised and bleeding, he clung to them peelers as if they were his dearest friends. If I close my eyes I can see the people jumping up, one behind another, and snarling with their teeth and making at him like the dogs you saw tonight after a rat. I can also still see the blood glistening in his hair and beard.

'The whores who had known Nancy best had worked their way into the centre of the crowd at the street corner and they spat at him and screamed out their encouragement to the screaming mob to tear out his god-forsaken heart. Those of us who escaped capture fled through a maze of close, narrow and muddy streets, thronged by the roughest and poorest of waterside people, to the upper room of a ruined house on Jacob's Island, beyond Dockhead in the borough of Southwark. As you know, at that time it was a rowdy hellhole of a place.'

I nodded my agreement. On Jacob's Island the wooden chambers of derelict warehouses rise like misshapen monsters out of the stinking water that runs from an inlet of the sewage-filled Thames. All the buildings have walls that are crumbling with decay and are encrusted with filth. Most have long since had their doors and windows removed, leaving behind just dark dirt-smeared black holes. Many lack even a roof. Here, amid the ruins and floating garbage, live only the most destitute in rooms so loathsome they beggar my power of description. It was here that Tommy and the others hoped to hide. They hoped to lose themselves amid the human refuse of the river — the ballast-heavers and coal-whippers, the petty touts and sharpers, the road-sweepers and beggars, the whores and ragged orphans, and the broken unemployed.

'In addition to Charley and me,' continued Tommy, 'there was Bill's mate, Toby Crackit, and a returned transport called Johnny Kags, who was one of the oldest of Fagin's associates. I told them all how I had seen the Jew captured and how the police officers had had to fight like devils to prevent the angry crowd seizing him and tearing him apart. I described how at one spot Fagin had fallen and how the police had been forced to make a ring around him and fight their way out. Whilst I was telling them this, you can imagine our surprise when Bull's-eye jumped through our window and fell panting at our feet. At first we assumed Bill had somehow escaped and had left the dog to make its own way to safety. We saw it was exhausted and we let it curl up at our feet and sleep. Our error was revealed when a couple of hours later Bill pounded at our door, demanding entry. Or rather his ghost did, for his face was ashen white, his eyes deep sunken, his cheeks hollow, and his flesh wasted. Whatever his crimes, we were ready to protect him, although, except perhaps for Toby, more from fear than friendship.

'At first Bill said little that made any sense. He appeared to be in a kind of daze. He wanted to know if Nancy was buried and, when we told him her body was still held by the police, he cried out that such an ugly thing as her crushed body should yet remain among the living. But gradually the wildness in his eyes grew less. He swore to us that he was innocent of Nancy's death and that he had returned rather than escaped because he was determined to discover her murderer. He said that he had not been able to sleep for three days because her ghost was haunting him and begging him to revenge her death. We believed him. All that is, except Charley, who had long regarded Nancy as a kind of sister. He screamed out that he'd rather be beaten to death or boiled alive than see Bill escape justice. Opening a window, he blew our cover, yelling 'Murder! Help!' at the top of his voice to attract attention before we could stop him. Bill attacked Charley, throwing him to the ground and pounding him with his hamlike fists. But the unequal contest did not last long for we heard the tramp of hurried feet crossing the wooden bridge that crossed the muddy inlet to our wretched house, and then loud knocking at our door and the ever-rising murmur of angry voices.

'Though badly bruised, Charley would not be silenced but yelled out again, 'Help! He's here! Break down the door!' Bill shook Charley like the bull terrier you saw this evening shook his rats. He repeatedly banged Charley's head against the wall till I thought it was a wonder his brains did not smear the wooden panelling. He then told us to throw the screeching Hell-babe into another room. Once this was done, he promptly locked the door. But the damage was done. Undaunted, Bill looked down on the ever-increasing mob surrounding the house and told them to do their worst because he'd cheat them yet. I shudder still at the resulting clamour that arose from the infuriated crowd. Some called to set the house on fire and burn us out, others called for sledgehammers to break down the door or ladders to enter through one of the windows. Some of the boldest even attempted to climb up the waterspout. Brave though I am, I don't mind admitting to you that sometimes I still hear the savage roar of their hatred in my nightmares.'

Chitling shuddered and paused to take a swig from a flask that he drew from his pocket. He offered the flask to me but I declined. Wiping his mouth with the back of his hand, he continued.

'You know the terrible outcome. Bill climbed out on to the roof, hoping to drop into the Folly Ditch by means of a long rope, and thence make his escape. The mob poured into the surrounding houses and climbed innumerable staircases so they could see him from every window and rooftop, venting their anger by shouting foul obscenities at him. Rich rewards were promised to anyone who could lay hold of him. He set his foot against the chimneystack and fastened one end of the rope firmly round it. Then he made a running noose, which he began to place over his body, but at the very instant when he brought the loop over his head previous to slipping it beneath his armpits, he lost his balance and tumbled over the parapet. The noose tightened round his neck as he fell for thirty-five feet. Bill yelled out Nancy's name. Then there was a sudden jerk, a terrible convulsion of his limbs, and there he hung, like a puppet on a string.'

He paused and took another drink from his flask.

'We listened to the jeering of the mob even as they gloated over his corpse. There was only one creature still faithful to him and that was Bull's-eye. It jumped after its master and dashed out its brains. Waste of a good dog, if you ask me. I vowed then that I'd seek a different life — one that wouldn't lead me to the treadmill, the oakum shed, or the hangman's noose.'

He paused again in his tale, this time because he heard the sounds of the rat-fighting reaching a crescendo below us. He gave me a furtive glance, which made his face even more unattractive, and looked to end the interview, saying he could tell me no more.

'Do you believe Bill was innocent?'

'I can tell you, Mr Twist, that Bill died not just yelling his defiance but protesting his innocence. It don't mean that he didn't kill her, but, unlike Charley Bates, I believe he was telling the truth. I think Nancy died at another's hands. Although Bill was dreadfully rough against her at times, especially when he had had too much to drink, he loved her. More than that, in his own strange way he worshipped Nancy. Passionately and whole-heartedly. And I think if he had killed her he would have escaped. After all, he had plenty of opportunity to do so. Ask yourself the questions the police never did. Why did he leave London and then return? Why, if subsequent accounts are to be believed, did he apparently spend hours traversing sections of the city and the surrounding countryside? Why did he enter into conversations about the murder in pubs and streets, risking drawing attention to himself? Why did he again leave the city only to return for a second time? Were those the actions of a guilty man or a man desperately trying to discover who had murdered the only person he had ever truly loved? I think I know which

145

I believe. So you see, Mr Twist, if I'm honest I am as certain as I can be that the real murderer of Nancy escaped the moment Bill died.'

I could tell that Tommy Chitling desperately wanted me to accept his ideas on Nancy's murder and I could see why he had never told Betsy. Had she heard his story, she would have moved heaven and earth to discover who had killed Nancy. I could see at first he doubted that I could ever see Bill in any but the worst light because he knew the reasons I had to hate the man who had so brutally terrorized me. Yet glancing at me again he was able to judge that I felt his questions had an undeniable validity. The silence between us was only broken by the sound of tables being thumped in the main bar. Tommy Chitling stood up to return to his duties and I accompanied him back into his pub. He grasped my hand and shook it more warmly, saying:

'If you want to try and verify what I've told you, then seek out Toby Crackit. I know he's still alive because I've seen him occasionally, but I've no idea where he lives. I am sure he will say the same as me. Bill did not kill Nancy. I suspect it's time for some different kind of rat-catching, Mr Twist, but you will have to identify your rat first. Mine won't answer your needs.'

9

Confirmation

For a few days after my meeting with Tommy Chitling I found it hard to sleep. My dreams were filled with images too horrible for me to describe as I wrestled with my memories of Bill Sikes. He had deliberately terrorized me from the moment we met. I have only to close my eyes and I can see him as clearly now in my imagination as I did in the flesh all those years ago. His broad heavy countenance and scowling eyes, the stubble that frequently covered his chin, the dirty belcher handkerchief round his neck, his black-velveteen coat and soiled drab breeches, his grey cotton stockings and lace-up half-boots. It was his blows and not just Nancy's lies that secured my return to Fagin's clutches. It was he who terrified me by threatening to allow his hellhound to tear me apart. It was his fist as well as the Jew's club that would have punished me had not Nancy intervened and protected me, receiving blows in my stead. Above all, it was Bill Sikes who took me on that terrifying housebreaking expedition that so nearly caused my death. Was I now to believe that this monster was innocent? And, if so, who had killed Nancy?

I am sure you can understand my reluctance to rely entirely on Tommy Chitling's account and so I determined to do as he said and seek out another witness of the events. Like him, it seemed to me that the obvious person to verify what I had been told would be Bill's closest associate, Toby Crackit, who was also present at Sikes's return. However, I knew that having a meeting with him was not going to be easy. How do you set about finding one man amid all the masses that crowd London? As you can imagine, days passed in fruitless enquiries and search. No one to whom I spoke knew anything about his whereabouts or, if they did, they had no intention of informing on him. As I knew to my cost, Crackit was not a man to be lightly crossed and violence was second nature to him.

It was for that reason that part of me was glad at my failure to find him. He was, after all, the man who had joined in the abortive burglary attempt and he had treated me as harshly as Sikes, threatening to murder me unless I did exactly what he wanted. I had all but given up hope of finding him when fate stepped in.

One night I was heading home after another wasted day and I walked along the New Cut, a rather notorious street market that stretches from Waterloo Road to Great Charlotte Street. It comprises hundreds of street stalls. These are lit mainly by grease lamps and it gives the place a strange glare, especially when the mist rises up from the dank streets. That evening as usual the air was thick with the sound of competing costers urging potential purchasers to buy their varied wares: 'Three a penny Yarmouth bloaters!' 'Who'll buy a bonnet?' 'Here's yer turnips!' 'Feel the quality!' 'Fine russets!' 'Pick 'em out cheap!' 'Chestnuts all 'ot!' 'What do you think of this here?' 'A penny a lot!' 'Get yer Lucifers!' and countless other cries. And amid all this babble I suddenly heard a gruff voice that I recognized shouting 'Fine warnuts! Sixteen a penny, fine war-r-nuts! Buy, buy, buy, buy, buy, bu-u-uy!' The last time I had heard that distinctive voice the words had been giving me orders to break into a house or else he'd crack open my head.

I looked for the source of the voice and there he was, Toby Crackit, armed this time not with a pistol and crowbar but with an innocuous large basket of walnuts, which he was attempting to sell without, as far as I could tell, much success. He was dressed in a filthy green-coloured coat with large brass buttons, a bright-red neckerchief, a shawl-pattern waistcoat, drab breeches, and unexceptionable boots. His face looked older, but otherwise he had not changed much and the little hair he had was still of a reddish dye and twisted into the long corkscrew curls that I remembered. Putting aside the revulsion that I felt towards him, I moved quickly over to where he was. His black eyes stared unmeaningfully at me but, pleased to have a customer at last, he offered me walnuts from his basket for sale.

'Don't you recognize me, Toby?' I said.

He looked more closely but clearly could not place me.

'I'm Oliver. Oliver Twist.'

'Fagin's lad?' he muttered in surprise, looking at the quality of my apparel and the smartness of my appearance. 'You appear to have done well. I always said yer mug would be a fortun' to ye.'

'I've not done bad for myself.'

'Down with innocence, eh?' He leered and gave a noiseless laugh. Then he muttered under his breath, 'I remember when you were less businesslike. What a dammed coward you were.' With unnerving accuracy he mimicked my childhood voice: 'O for God's sake let me go! Let me run away and die in the fields! O pray have mercy on me and do not make me steal. For the love of all the bright angels in Heaven have mercy!' Then he spat on to the cobbles to show his disgust. 'I'm glad to see you're game enough now.'

I recoiled at his assumption that any money I had must stem from ill-gotten gains and, priglike, I replied: 'My wealth has nothing to do with crime, and I'm prepared to use it to see justice done.'

His face clouded over at this pompous response and he looked around, fearing doubtless that I had possibly come to ensure his arrest. Sensing that he was about to flee, I firmly grasped his arm and, before he could retaliate, pleaded my case:

'Believe me, I've no interest in you, Toby. What happened in the past between you and me is water under the bridge as far as I am concerned. All I want is justice for Nancy and to know the truth about Bill Sikes's role in her murder.'

'There's no point going over all that. What's dead is dead. Nancy deserved to die and Bill got no justice.'

'It may surprise you, Toby, but I have reason to think you might be right. I've a little evidence that has led me to believe Bill might not have killed Nancy, but not enough to be certain. You and Bill were mates so don't you owe it to him to tell me what really happened, especially if he was innocent?'

'Ay, Bill and I were mates, sure enough. The best of mates.'

He hesitated, struggling with a mixture of emotions, and then, with his usual devil-may-care swagger, he beckoned me to follow him down a nearby alleyway. Regardless of the danger, I followed and soon found myself being led into a far from salubrious small brewing-place at the end of a dark and damp passage. I ordered drinks and we entered its backyard to sit at a table where we could not be overheard. He dropped his basket of walnuts on to the grimy floor, then ran his brown-stained fingers, ornamented with large common rings, through his tangled locks before drinking deeply from his mug. I looked at the beverage in front of me and decided it was safer not to try its contents. He smiled, doubtless remembering how he had tried to force me to drink when I was a child. Wiping his mouth with the back of his hand, Crackit reopened our conversation:

'Times is bad at present, otherwise you would not find me here. This warnut selling is just to tide me over. Back to me beginnings you might say, because me and Bill were both brought up as plucky coster boys. My father was a wagoner who worked the country roads but he died whilst I was still a young 'un. My mother took up with a new man and, as soon as I could shout loud enough, he put me to work in the markets from four in the morning till nine at night. Today I've not managed to sell much but then, on a good day, I could sell twelve bushel of fruit in a day. That's when I first met Bill. He was dressed flash and up to all the tricks. He taught me quite a few. He'd boil oranges and prunes to make 'em swell and look bigger, put cabbage leaves under a layer of strawberries in his pottles, and mix three sieves of indiff'rent foreign cherries with one sieve of good English ones.'

'Given what has happened, it's a pity he did not stick to such minor offences rather than turning to violent crime,' I replied.

'You have to understand, Oliver, violence comes natural. You nivver knew Bill's father but, believe me, he made Bill look soft. And as coster boys, we learnt to work our fists well, 'cos anyone avoiding a fight was laughed at. We was teached to bear pain without complaining or flinching. You might not believe it but anyone without money would say to a pal, 'Give us a penny and yer can take a punch at me nose,' and many a time Bill and I have sparred for just a beer or even a lark. We were so good at fighting we could muzzle half a dozen bobbies before breakfast if we wished. If you've got a talent you have to use it — and that's wot me and Bill did.'

I had cause to remember how 'handy' both men were with their fists and it did not surprise me that they had increasingly turned to criminal activities. 'Tell me about Nancy,' I said.

'What's there to say that you don't know? Gals are there for the taking and Nancy was one of the best, even if she was at times a spitfire. Her trade was useful too. If money were tight, she could earn us a few meals by serving others, if you take me meaning. And in Nancy's case the good thing was she couldn't conceive any chance children, 'cos she was barren.'

His words should not have shocked me. I know all too well the amoral way of life of costers and thieves. Eating, drinking, gambling, and the occasional visit to a theatre or dance are what usually dominates their lives and they are unrestrained in their sexual behaviour. Why should they know any different? They lack any education and, unless they are fortunate to experience genuine Christian compassion, few have any acquaintance with Christianity other than to be occasionally subjected to some stupid, well-meaning person trying to foist a religious tract upon them — an entirely pointless exercise as virtually all of them are unable to read! In this part of London it is probably fair to say that not three or four in a hundred have ever been inside a church or any place of worship and they know nothing of Christ but to use his name as a swear word. Their lives are in every sense truly godless. No, his words should not have shocked me and yet I could not stop myself recoiling at Crackit's unfeeling and callous attitude.

'It's not my definition of loving a woman to use and abuse her,' I told him. 'I keep hearing that Bill loved Nancy but I saw no love in any of his actions. He did not even ever offer her marriage.'

'What's the point of wedlock when a pair can be together and no one gives a damn? There's precious few bother around here. It's just a waste of money. Bill luvved her and she luvved him. That was enough for them both.'

'And the ill-treatment? I know how frequently Bill hit her.'

'Nancy usually deserved it and women seem to like men better for beating 'em. It's been my experience that as long as the bruises hurt, women will think only of the chap who gave them. It's the same with dogs. Treat 'em mean and they do exactly what's wanted. That's why Bill's dog was such a terror when Bill used to put 'im to fight other dogs in tap-rooms and backyards. Many a good bit of cash Bull's-eye won us when he was in his heyday. Mind you, I'd have wrung its neck had I known its stupid following of Bill would lead to his discovery and death.'

'But Bill did not kill Nancy?'

'Lord no. Bill weren't afraid of murder but I've told ye he luvved her. In all the hue and cry after she was found dead, me and Tommy Chitling and that old returned transport Johnny Kags took refuge together. You can imagine our surprise when Bull's-eye jumps in at the open winder, covered with mud and half-lame, but we assumed Bill had long since gone and left him. However, Bill afterwards turned up, banging at our door. The others were all for keeping him out but I insisted we let him in. It was me who opened the door and I hardly recognized him. It was not just that the lower part of his face was hidden partly by three days' growth of beard and partly by his handkerchief. The truth was he was more like the ghost of Sikes than me old mate. He was a ghastly white colour and his cheeks were drawn, his eyes sunken, and his body wasted. He feared we might not let him stay because of the danger of harbouring him, but I told him he could stop till he thought it safe.

Bill swore his innocence over Nancy's death and told us he'd come back and risked his life so he could catch the real killer. That's the God's truth and I believed him. A mate does not lie to a mate. But then that stupid loud-mouthed Charley Bates arrived and began shouting out 'Murder!' and 'Down with him!' Bill grabbed him by the throat and tried to silence him, repeating to him what he had told us, that he had not been responsible in any way for Nancy's murder. Charley wouldn't listen and, when some peelers arrived to investigate the noise, he managed to free himself sufficiently to scream out once again, urging them to break down the door. Bill had to make 'is way out quick by climbing up on the roof — and you know the rest.'

Here was the confirmation I wanted that Tommy Chitling had indeed told me the truth. Bill really had not killed Nancy. The question was whether Crackit knew who had.

'Who killed her, Toby?'

'I wish I knew, 'cos he wouldn't live long if I got hold of him. I've given the matter plenty of thought over the past few years but, if you want the truth, I'm no wiser now than I was then. You see, Bill gave us no clue. I'm not sure even he knew what had happened to her.'

'But surely you must have some ideas of your own?'

'The only thing that's crossed my mind since is that Charley seemed very quick to want Bill caught. His screams almost did for all of us and certainly did for Bill. I think it's just possible Charley might have had his own reasons for wanting Bill out of the way? If so, he might know more about what really happened to Nancy.'

'It's an interesting thought. The rest of you clearly accepted Bill's account of his innocence. Why did Charley alone insist on believing he was Nancy's murderer? It is indeed possible that he had his own reasons for wanting Bill wrongly hanged for her murder. Why have you not followed this up with him?'

'For the simple reason I've not been able to find Charley since that day. I can assure you he's not anywhere here in London, or else by now I'd have found him. The story is that he headed up north. No one's heard of him since.'

My search for the truth seemed to be blocked once more. Searching London was bad enough but searching the entire country was beyond what was possible. I realized I would have to look for other leads than Charley Bates to help me discover the truth. I hastily slipped Crackit some money in acknowledgement of his time and took my leave. As I left, he shouted after me:

'If you find out who killed her, let me know and I'll see justice done, no questions asked. Nancy was a fine gal and Bill was me best mate. I don't forgit me old mates.'

10

Bumble's Story

After Toby Crackit had confirmed Tommy Chitling's version of events, I decided my best chance lay in seeking out another of my childhood monsters to see if he could cast any light on my origins and therefore on the tragic events which had led to Nancy's death. I knew it would not be easy to trace the whereabouts of Mr Bumble but I felt that he perhaps offered me the one real chance of shedding some further light on my ancestry. I knew he and his equally abominable wife had been deprived of their positions as workhouse masters because of their deception and crimes. Mr Dickens had taken some delight in recording how they became paupers in the very institution they had once run and so my enquiries naturally started there. However, I found that their stay there had been a short one because, like many of the destitute, they were soon moved on.

You will understand that seeking a homeless person in London is like searching for a needle in a haystack, but one that is

160

seething with corruption and disease. There were times when I almost gave up the task especially as my search led me to places whose foulness defied belief. I started to think that even the pernicious Mr Bumble did not deserve to end his days amid such soul-consuming wretchedness. But, as with Toby Crackit, my perseverance eventually paid dividends.

When at last I traced his whereabouts, I discovered that he was scraping an existence in a foul district, which was hopelessly ill-drained. The rotting floors of the houses rested on soil that had absorbed every kind of soluble filth. Alongside the houses was a stagnant lake thickened by human excrement. On its surface floated dead cats and dogs exhibiting every stage of disgusting decomposition. The whole area round about had become like a gigantic putrid sponge. The buildings themselves were stained with every indescribable hue that long exposure to the weather, damp, and rottenness can impart to tenements built of the roughest and cheapest materials. Although the place was not a thieves' stronghold, because its rubbish-strewn streets were not sufficiently narrow, I remained on my guard because the area's many arched passage-openings lent themselves to ambush. It was no place for a stranger to wander about, especially after dusk when the only light came from the handful of candles that here and there flickered behind translucent blinds to announce beds for any travellers fortunate enough to afford them.

I eventually found the house where I had been told I would find Mr Bumble situated off a fairly wide slum courtyard, which was covered with mud and slime. It was cluttered with coster carts and water-barrels containing water that looked little better than that in the nearby lake. Poles on which to dry clothes hung from every casement, but the tattered and soot-covered garments that hung from them seemed scarce worth the dismal effort. In the moistly crumbling walls of the courtyard open doorways gaped where doors had been long since removed for firewood. At some of these unwholesome entrances children crouched like maggots in a mouldy cheese, their faces aged before their time and their bodies warped and misshapen by a mixture of cruelty and neglect. A number of prostitutes of the poorest sort lay sprawled asleep in some of the other doorways, some partly exposing their naked charms to any beholder. In the yard itself half-drunken hags checked themselves in the midst of pots of beer or pints of gin to see whether I was a prospective customer and to yell out what they were prepared to offer in return for a pittance. Sounds of drunkenness and quarrelling issued from windows that had mostly been reduced to containing only fragments of glass.

The house I wanted still had, amazingly, its large green entrance door, though it was worm-eaten and hanging from its hinges and smeared with excrement and indescribable other filth. I moved towards it, avoiding the evil-smelling gutter that ran across the courtyard and watching carefully where I trod on the uneven pavement to avoid garbage and worse.

Undeterred I entered, conscious that I might be placing not only my possessions but my life in danger by entering such a place. An ill-lit passageway led to a kitchen filled with a fog of smoke through which the sunlight from a hole in the roof cut a narrow shaft. The beams that hung down from the roof and ran from wall to wall were blackened by the smoke, as was the flue of the chimney, which stood out from the bare brick wall like a begrimed buttress. The windows were patched with stiffened paper and stuffed with the foulest rags. A rude iron gas pipe stood in the centre of the room to offer additional light, whilst a wooden bench projected from each of its walls.

In front of this primitive seating were ranged a series of tables on which rested a number of dozing men. Some inmates were grouped round the fire. Some were kneeling to toast herrings, of which the place smelt strongly, while others were drying the ends of cigars they had picked from the streets. A few were simply drying out themselves and the smell of vomit and urine from their foul clothing did little to enhance the polluted atmosphere of the kitchen.

The men were as motley and ragged an assemblage as I had ever seen. Their hair was matted like sheep's wool, their skin sallow and in many instances showing signs of infection, and their chins were grimy with their unshorn beards. The ill-fitting rags that acted as their clothing had obviously been collected from the city's refuse and they were so filthy that it was virtually impossible to discern their original colour. Some were in smock-frocks, some in waistcoats that had long ceased to be fashionable, and others in strange unidentifiable motley costumes. A few had acquired striking if dirty garb. One was dressed in what looked like an old military jacket but which had wooden buttons, another wore what I could only imagine had originated in a circus, while a third had on his feet an incongruous pair of lady's lace-sided boots, the toes of which had been cut off so that he might get them on.

Some of the men appeared pitiable in their poverty, but others scowled in such a manner as to leave me in doubt as to whether they had any of their humanity left within them. And on the bench at the furthest end of the kitchen was one whose squalor and wretchedness produced only nausea in me. His eyes were sunk deep in his face, his stubbled cheeks were drawn in, and his nostrils were pinched with evident want. His clothes were black and shiny at every fold with grease, and they hung on his skeleton frame like a loose bag. I had never beheld so gaunt a picture of famine. And this living scarecrow was Mr Bumble.

I sent for some meat to be placed on the table before him, and, with a glance at me, he dipped his nose in the plate and then began painfully tearing the food asunder with his arthritic fingers before slowly chewing it between gums that had long since lost most of their teeth. When he had finished, I looked at him and asked him whether he dared ask me for more. He looked at me most warily and then I saw that he gradually recognized who his unexpected benefactor was. In a weak voice far removed from the bellow that had so terrified me as a child, Mr Bumble croaked his welcome.

'Is it really, you, Master Oliver? It's many a year since we met and you've become such a fine young gentleman.' He grimaced in what he took to be a friendly smile but which to any onlooker bore more resemblance to a corrupt leer, and then he added, 'Mr Limbkins got it wrong when he said one day you'd be hung.'

My mind went back to our first meeting when I was a mere boy and he came to fetch me from Mrs Mann's cottage and place me in the workhouse. Mr Bumble then had been a very different figure, fat and choleric and proud of his position as beadle of the parish. He had shown no sympathy for the frightened little creature I then was, but paraded me before the workhouse board like a pariah.

When, driven by hunger and the threats of the other boys, I had dared ask for a second helping of the thin and meagre gruel provided for our nourishment, it had been Mr Bumble who had willingly seen to my punishment, repeatedly applying the cane and plunging me into dark and solitary confinement. He had taken cruel pleasure in telling me I was a bastard orphan whom nobody could ever love. And when he sold me to one of his friends, Mr Sowerberry, so I could become the undertaker's slave, and I wept with fear, he again showed not an ounce of pity for a desperately lonely boy. He simply told me I was one of the most ungrateful and worst-disposed lads he had ever known.

It came as no surprise that when I attacked Noah Claypole, Sowerberry's assistant, because of his cruel and vicious taunts, it was Mr Bumble who returned to sadistically beat me with the parochial cane and urge starvation as a method of bringing me under control. 'Meat, ma'm, meat,' he had roared at Mrs Sowerberry, 'You've overfed him, ma'am. You've raised a artificial soul and spirit in him, ma'am, unbecoming a person of his condition. If you had kept the boy on gruel it would never have happened.'

Mr Bumble interrupted my reverie as he tried to ingratiate himself by rewriting history. 'I always had your interests at heart, Master Oliver,' he mumbled. He reached out to grasp my hand. I could not help recoiling from his skeletal touch and, sick though he was, he recognized my obvious distaste. 'Come now, Master Oliver, you owe more to me than you think. If it had not been for me and my late wife you would never have come into your inheritance.' I looked at his frame, so obviously nearing extinction, and wondered how the calculating greed I saw in his face could fire up so fiercely. Did he not realize how close he was to meeting his Maker and being held to account for all his actions? He witnessed my instinctive abhorrence and muttered defensively: 'When a man's lost his position, he may as well go the whole hog, bristles and all, and this low lodging is the entire pig.'

'Tell me all that you know about my ancestry and your part in my becoming Mr Brownlow's heir and I will see you are suitably rewarded,' I replied.

Mr Bumble clutched my arm and whispered, 'The truth is not always to our liking, Master Oliver.'

I stared into his rheumy eyes and said coldly, 'It is only the truth I now want to hear. If I detect one lie in what you say, expect nothing from me.' Seeing my resolve, he proceeded to tell me what I had most feared to hear.

'Whatever airs you give yourself now, I can tell you you are not, and therefore never were, the child of Agnes Fleming, although you grew up with him who was and you looked not dissimilar to him. Agnes Fleming never even knew you because she died giving him birth. She bequeathed to the child who had killed her a gold locket, although he never received it. As you know, Martha, the nurse who attended her deathbed, stole it along with her wedding ring. Believe me, Master Oliver, your wretched mother was a very different kind of woman from Agnes Fleming. All she bequeathed to you was a distinguishing birthmark on your back. If she felt any love for you, it had to be suppressed because she was forced to hand you over to the workhouse so she could simply continue her whoring ways.'

'Then I am Nancy's child?' I sobbed.

'Yes, and she was precious quick to realize that when you entered Fagin's lair. Nancy was a very clever girl, sometimes too clever for her own good. She came to the workhouse to make sure that you were the child she had been forced to relinquish when she was little more than a child herself. In the process she spoke to Martha, who was then near to death. It was Nancy who first heard the story of the beautiful Agnes and her rich but absent lover. It was Nancy who persuaded Martha to seek forgiveness for her actions before she died by handing over the locket and wedding ring to Mrs Corney, the matron of the workhouse. It was Nancy who persuaded Mrs Corney and me to pretend Agnes's child was you, promising us that, once the father had been found, there would be money in it for us all.

'The arrival of Monks played into her hands. Foolish and susceptible man that he was, it was easy for us to make him believe you were his long-lost half-brother. Twenty-five sovereigns he paid me and Mrs Corney — or rather Mrs Bumble, as she had become. That was a less good bargain! I paid a heavy price the day I married her. I sold myself for six teaspoons, a pair of sugar-tongs, and a milk-pot; with a small quantity of second-hand furniture, and twenty pound in money. I went very reasonable. Cheap, dirt cheap! She never understood that it is the prerogative of a woman to obey her husband and she had the nerve not only to shout abuse at me if I disagreed with her but also to assault my person, scratching my face and tearing my hair. She so shamed me in front of the paupers that I lost any authority I once had.

'The one consolation in my current condition is that I am finally rid of the harridan. You see, Oliver, the only good thing about workhouses is that they separate man and wife and the workhouse has now seen to her for good. Starved her good and proper it did, till her harsh voice wasn't more than a whisper and she lay dying. When I heard the news, I pleaded to be allowed to see her. I think the authorities were touched by my desire, not realizing that all I wanted was an opportunity to gloat over her.

'They granted my wish and I had the joy of

seeing her skeleton figure in the bed, covered only with a poor patchwork coverlet. I was the worst thing she wanted to see and she tried to raise her feeble and emaciated arms to ward me off, but the effort proved too great. I leant over her and whispered. The nurse thought I was saying a loving farewell, but in fact I was portraying to her all the delights of the hell that I was sure awaited her. She gasped her last with my curses ringing in her ears. Since then I've often puzzled as to how such a cruel place could, over this matter of disposing of a wife, be so kind!'

Mr Bumble's pleasure at whatever memories of his wife's suffering he had evoked in his mind made him temporarily lose the thread of his story. His breath became ragged, his face turned even more deathlike, and his eyes lost their focus. I shook the frail body, yelling at him to tell me more if he wanted some money as a reward. In desperation I thrust a few coins in his hand and, villain that he was, the touch of the metal on his palm was sufficient to bring him back to the present.

He wiped away some of the dribble from his mouth and muttered, 'Monks was a fool, Oliver. He paid us to lead him by the nose. It was so funny to see the pleasure he obtained when we dropped the evidence of your supposed birth into the river. He had not the slightest suspicion of how much he was being duped. The beauty of the plan was that it was Monks' actions in seeking your destruction that gave such weight to the view that you must be Agnes Fleming's child, reinforced by poor Mr Brownlow's mistaken opinion that you and the portrait of her were so alike. As I said, in looks you were not dissimilar to Agnes's child. It was Nancy, of course, who betrayed Monks' existence to both Mr Dickens and Mr Brownlow, as well as to Rose Maylie.'

'But, why did you not tell Mr Brownlow this when he faced you with plotting with Monks?' I asked.

'Think of all that had happened, Master Oliver. Nancy was dead and Monks was a spineless wreck. We feared what action might be taken against us if we admitted the deception, especially as by then Agnes's real child was dead. And dead because of the treatment received at our hands.'

Even as I asked who the child was, I knew the answer Mr Bumble would give me. It was Dick, my sole friend and playmate in the workhouse where we both had been so cruelly treated. We had been whipped and starved and shut up together many and many a time.

Dick's pale face had been the only one I had wanted to see after fleeing from Mr Sowerberry's before I set out for London. Through the gates of the workhouse Dick had thrust out his pale emaciated arm to touch me.

'You mustn't say you saw me, Dick,' I had told him. 'I am running away. They beat and ill-use me, Dick, and I am going to seek my fortune some long way off. I don't know where. How pale you are!'

'I heard the doctor tell them I was dying,' he had replied with a faint smile. 'I am very glad to see you one last time, but don't stop, don't stop.'

'No, I won't stop but I wanted to say goodbye to you before I left. I promise you that I shall see you again, Dick. I know I shall! Don't talk of dying. I'll make my fortune and then return to make sure you can leave here and be well and happy!'

'I hope so, but I think your good fortune will happen after I am dead and not before. I know the doctor must be right, Oliver, because I dream so much of Heaven and angels and kind faces that I never see when I am awake.'

With what little energy he had, Dick had climbed up the low gate and flung his little arms around my neck. 'Kiss me,' he whispered. And as we kissed he offered the first blessing I had ever had on my head: 'Goodbye, Oliver! God bless you!'

I now knew that in seeking to advance her son's interests, Nancy had helped deny the birthright of my one true childhood friend and, in the process, had doomed his guiltless soul to an early death. Thrusting a handful of gold coins into Mr Bumble's palm as the tears filled my eyes, I stumbled away from his rotting, hateful presence. Judging from the commotion as I left the room, I suspect that those around him ensured he soon lost the coins I had given him by depriving him of the little life his skeletal body still retained. But I cared not what happened to Mr Bumble. My thoughts lay entirely with my childhood companion who for my sake had been so cruelly condemned.

11

The Mystery Remains

The fact that I was Nancy's child did not resolve the mystery of her death. However, it gave me the courage to confide the result of my investigations to Rose Maylie. Supposing me to be her nephew, she had lovingly lavished so much interest and affection on me that I cared for her more than any other living soul. I hated the idea that I might cause her any distress by my revelations but I felt she had to know that I was not the love child of her weak and erring sister, Agnes. Nevertheless, the decision to inform her was not an easy one because I feared to risk the end of our loving relationship. Rose had forgiven her sister's crime of passion, but I doubted she would find it so easy to accept me as the bastard son of a common whore, even if, all those years ago, she had shown such concern for Nancy's well-being. All I could offer in my real mother's defence was that her devotion to me was unquestionable. After all, she had been prepared to commit any act to rescue me from the brutalities of the life that she

175

herself had suffered.

Rose and Harry Maylie resided in a pretty village, which at the time of these events was still just on the outskirts of London. Sadly it has now been totally enveloped by the all-encompassing urban sprawl of our metropolis. Their pretty house stood on the corner of an ancient common so that, although it was approached through a growing sprawl of new housing, its immediate surroundings were woody lanes and, beyond these, the eye could gaze upon open meadowland, the haunt of skylarks. It was a low, thatched affair, its walls old and weather-stained, its casements full of richly coloured geraniums, and its most prominent feature a large bow-window to the right of its oaken door, framed by clematis on one side and a climbing rose on the other. I had come to regard this small picturesque place as almost a second home and the very image of comfort and content. It had a fragrant flower-filled garden, full of hollyhocks, roses, honeysuckles, and fruit trees of all sorts so that to my eye it was a second Eden.

As a sickly child I had exchanged the horrors of the workhouse and of Fagin's den for the beauties of the Maylie's garden. It was as if I had been transported from Hell to Heaven and I shall always associate Rose with the beauty of her flowers. Even Charles

Dickens failed to write an adequate account not only of the pleasure and delight but also of the peace of mind I found in that rural idyll. The rose and honeysuckle clung to the cottage walls, the ivy crept around the trunks of the trees, and the garden flowers perfumed the air with delicious scents. When I looked out of the house I loved to watch Mrs Maylie and Rose working together to tend their paradise, I listened with pleasure to all they said. And each morning I would rise early and roam the nearby fields, plundering the hedges, far and wide, for nosegays of wild flowers to embellish her breakfast table.

Time and a change of residence had not diminished Rose's ability to make her garden a haven of tranquillity and, as a man, I had often sat with Rose amid this house's special sweet-scented beauty and whiled away the hours, especially remembering those friends we had lost. It was within its beauty that I had confided most of my sorrow at Mr Brownlow's death and Rose, blessed angel that she was, had done much to ease my path during the darkest days of my mourning. Now I had to speak of an equal grief, yet the day seemed unaware of my new-found gloom. There was scarce a cloud to dapple the deep-blue sky, aglow with sunshine that burnished the blossoms all around me, and made the view over hill and dale and rich woodland one glorious vista of nature at its fairest and best.

I paused for a moment to smell once more the perfumed air before knocking at the oaken front door for admittance. It was opened by faithful Brittles, who had served the family since he was a lad and who had come close to murdering me all those years ago when Sikes had used me to break into their home. He greeted me with his usual delight, took my overcoat, told me I was warmly expected and led me into the parlour, which was the scene of the smiling and untiring discharge of much of Rose's domestic duties. Rose's welcome was as warm as it had ever been. Her simple goodness radiated through her every look and glance, and, not surprisingly, I felt the years had treated her kindly.

To my eyes she was almost exactly the same in appearance as when we had first met and she was just a young girl of seventeen radiating an artless loveliness. The only difference now was that motherhood had made her a little more rounded in shape and the early death of one of her children had made her a little wiser and perhaps a little less naïve. It pained me to risk bringing any fresh shadows into her life but I felt I had no choice. The honesty she expected from all those around her demanded that I should no longer let her live a lie. At an earlier meeting I had already intimated to her husband, Harry, the gist of what I wanted to tell her, and I relied on his common sense to support her through whatever pain I caused. Harry had taken time off from his work to ensure that he could attend our meeting. He had grown physically stouter and his thinning hair made him appear older, but he too was remarkably unchanged. Nobility of heart and mind does not always show itself physically, but in their case it did, and, if ever a couple's love and inherent kindness prevented the cruel marks of time, it was so with them.

Harry had told his wife that I was coming to give her some news relating to my family. He had arranged for their children to be taken out for the day by some friends. As you can imagine, Rose was anxious to hear my news. For my part I was less keen to communicate what I had discovered of my ancestry because, now that the moment had come, I feared even more the potential outcome on our relationship. I thought the likely result would be that she would never again permit me to cross her threshold.

'Rose,' I said, 'do you remember what I promised you when I was a child?'

'You promised me many things, Oliver.'

'I said that I wanted only to work for you and to give you pleasure by watering your flowers and watching your birds and running up and down for you the whole day long to make you happy. I'm not sure that I ever kept that promise in the way my childish heart had hoped, but now I must say things that will diminish your happiness. It is my hope that you will pardon me for the pain I must cause you, but, if that is not the case, I will understand.'

Rose looked alarmed, not only at my words but at my obvious discomposure. She grasped my hand and sought to reassure me, saying, 'Nothing you can say can undo the love we share, Oliver. Surely you must know that.'

Strengthened by this, I commenced my tale, informing her of the result of my investigations. It was not an easy task and I am not ashamed to say I shed tears in the telling. When I had finished, her soft blue eyes looked at me so strangely, then she shuddered, turning her face slightly away from me. Harry, good and true as ever, took one of her trembling hands and, anxious to comfort her, pressed it to his lips. To my eyes she seemed unable to register even his concern. I could sense the shock she had sustained and I cannot describe the agony that reaction caused within my breast. I now believed the revelation of my pedigree could have but one outcome. She would disown any future acquaintance with me. My heart felt as if it were about to break. I looked to take my leave, but Harry quietly signalled me to stay. I acknowledged my consent and we both stood awaiting her to voice her grief.

After what seemed an interminable silence she said, 'I can see your resemblance to her, Oliver, and it grieves me because now I cannot hide from the fact that your mother was a consummate liar. She entirely convinced me that she was speaking the truth when she came to see Mr Brownlow and me. Now I must question whether I will ever be able to trust my judgement again. Nancy told me how much she hated her life and how painful she found it that, because of her life of ill-repute, even the poorest women fell back before her as she made her way along a crowded pavement. She said her whole life had been spent in the midst of cold and hunger and riot and drunkenness and that she could expect to die only in the gutter. And when I pitied her, she thanked me for my kindness and blessed me for my goodness. After she told me you were Edwin Leeford's illegitimate son and of the plots of Fagin and Monks against you, I begged her to seek safety with us, but, with tears in her eyes, she told me it was too late for her to turn from her life of sin and sorrow and that she could not desert the man she loved. It pains me to say it but, yes, what an amazing actress she was, Oliver.

'When Mr Brownlow and I met her in the mist on London Bridge, she was exactly as you would have expected an informer to be. She was restless in her gestures, agitated in her manner, afraid to speak out on the public road lest we be overheard. The information we required to seize hold of Monks had to be dragged out of her, detailed though her description of him was. She convinced us she was in fear of her life. She said she had nightmares in which she was surrounded by bloody shrouds and felt the fires of hell burning her. She told us she had tried reading a book, but every page had the word 'coffin' writ large upon it. We offered her asylum, either in England or abroad, but she told us she was chained to her old life and had gone too far to turn back. Her only escape would be to throw herself, like many before her, into the river. Looking back, her every move, her every gesture, her every word was calculated to win our sympathy and our hearts.'

I replied to her: 'I am not so sure that it was all acting, Rose. Do not forget that within hours of that meeting, she lay bludgeoned to death. Maybe some of her fears were genuine.' I paused, wondering whether I should speak of what Betsy had told me. Then I took the plunge, saying, 'My mother believed that someone had tried to kill at least three of the people around her and that she might be next. One of those whom she believed to have been endangered was you. She thought your illness was due to poisoning. Was it? And, if so, who could have been responsible? I ask because I believe the same person may have been Nancy's murderer. You see, I am no longer sure that Bill Sikes killed her.'

Rose was visibly startled by my words and took some time to reflect before answering my questions. Then she said, 'I do not think I can help you, Oliver. All I can say is that the cause of my illness was certainly very mysterious and very sudden. I remember I had been in such high spirits that I and my dear mama — for that is what Harry's mother became to me — had been for a long walk. There was a brilliant moon and a light wind had sprung up that was unusually refreshing. When we returned I was still not tired and so I began to play the piano. Suddenly and inexplicably I became very downcast and began weeping inconsolably. The blood drained from my face and I began to feel very ill. Hot and cold flushes swept over me. Mama immediately sent me to my bed and summoned medical assistance. And that's all I remember. I was later told that I had nearly died and that only mama's prompt sending for medical help saved me.'

Harry, who had sat patiently while we spoke, gently grasped his wife's hand and kissed her cheek. 'I don't like to be reminded, dear, of how close I came to losing you, but this may be important. On the walk, did you eat or drink anything unusual?'

Rose pondered for what seemed an eternity, but was in reality no more than a few minutes. At last she said, 'Now I think back there was one possible way I might have been poisoned. I drank a small glass of milk which I thought was offered in kindness by a friendly young chap, whom we met outside a public house on our return journey.' She saw the look of triumph in my eyes as I urged her to describe him. 'It's a long time ago, Oliver, and we met but for a brief moment. All I can recall is that he was lively and good-humoured and reasonably though not well dressed. He was sitting outside having a drink as we passed by and he greeted us most politely and asked if we could give him directions, as he was a stranger to the area.

We obliged and chatted to him for a short while. I cannot remember much of what we said, although I do seem to think some of it was about Mr Dickens' serializations and what a good storywriter he was. He was then just becoming very fashionable and the young man was obviously a devotee. He offered to buy us refreshments. Mama declined but I said I would be grateful for a small glass of milk if the inn could provide such a drink. He went inside and returned with one. I drank it, thanked him for his kindness, and we said our goodbyes.'

Excitedly I stood up from my chair and said to them both, 'Then I believe Nancy was right and you, Rose, were poisoned alongside Bill Sikes and Mary Hogarth. Dickens fell out with my unfortunate mother because he believed her guilty of Mary's death, but I now think he got that wrong. Nancy had no part in Mary Hogarth's death. She had no reason to bear any grudge against her and she had every reason to not risk endangering her relationship with Dickens. But I am at a loss to know what I can do about finding out the truth now. I have sought the help of every likely person to get thus far in my investigations.' I looked my former confidante in the eye and added, 'Rose, if I may still call you that, all I can do is thank you for your past friendship and kindness and render my apologies that your kindness to the bastard son of a whore ever endangered your life.'

Harry grasped my arm and gasped, 'Oliver, how can you say such a thing!' A glance at his wife seemed to confirm his thoughts and he spoke the words I had feared would never be said, telling me that, although I was not Rose's nephew, I was still their dear, dear friend:

'Oliver, you know I fell in love with Rose although her own history was shrouded with some mystery. You know I willingly married her even when I knew her sister had proved a weak and fallen creature. I have never regretted for a moment either action. No wife could have been more loving or more devoted. She is my dearest companion and friend and the most loving mother of our children. We have both known you since you were but a small boy and we loved you for yourself. Just because we wrongly thought you were Agnes's child, does that mean we should turn our backs on you, who have been a friend for so many years and who have been more sinned against than sinning? We would be poor friends and worse Christians if we did that.'

He held out his hand and I am not ashamed to say my eyes filled with tears both at his words and at this sign of their continuing friendship. I shook his hand most warmly. Rose got up from her chair and threw her arms around us both. When our emotions were more under control, Harry was the first to speak and his words astounded me.

'Oliver, I have a vested interest in trying to discover who almost killed Rose. The memory of those dark days of her illness still sometimes haunts me in my dreams. I know of one person who just may be able to help us. A few weeks ago I was hearing a court case in my capacity as a magistrate. One of the witnesses was a man whom I recognized. At first I could not place where I had seen him before, but then it came to me. He was one of the men who gave evidence at the trial against Fagin. I imagine his knowledge of what happened in those last few weeks is probably unmatched. A few enquiries with my friends in the police and I am sure they will tell me where he can be found. I gather this man is often used by them as an informer.'

I was excited by his news. It seemed to me to offer fresh hope of further information. Although I stayed to share a meal with them, it is pointless describing to you the speculations in which we indulged for the rest of that day until their children returned and happier matters took over our conversation. Suffice it to say that none of us came remotely near guessing the truth that I ultimately discovered. Far more successful were Harry's subsequent enquiries through his acquaintance with Charles Field, the newly appointed chief of the Detective Department at Scotland Yard. This sagacious inspector, respected and feared throughout the city, agreed to see me and put me in touch with the man Harry had remembered.

My visit to Scotland Yard was a brief one. Field was a middle-aged man of portly presence, with a husky voice and a large, moist, knowing eye. He had a habit of emphasizing his conversation by the aid of a corpulent forefinger, which was constantly in juxtaposition with his eyes or nose. He introduced me to three of his sergeants, all of whom looked very respectable men. There was nothing lounging or slinking in their manners and they all greeted me warmly. Straw was a little wiry man of meek demeanour but strong sense. Whicher, who was thicker-set and marked with the small-pox, had a reserved and thoughtful air, as if he were engaged in some complicated mental arithmetic. Thornton, who had a ruddy face and a high, sunburnt forehead, had an air of keen observation though he looked the oldest. Together these policemen listened to some of my story, though I was careful to tell them as little as possible that might lower me in their estimation.

Though they sensed that I was holding back much of the truth behind my search, they were happy to provide me with the information I sought because of my connection to the Maylies. I was told the man whom Harry had recognized was Morris Bolter, alias Noah Claypole. It was a name that, as you will by now recognize, only served to bring back very unhappy memories. Apparently this taunter of orphans, deceiver of women, and coward among men had turned police informer and was therefore well known to all of them. I tried to hide my disquiet while Field provided the necessary details of his whereabouts. All the policeman asked in return was that I did not reveal the extent of Noah's work for them. Harry told me he would make the necessary arrangements for me to meet Claypole through his police contacts and I agreed to pay whatever price Noah wanted for any information he could provide.

As I left them I knew I did not relish a meeting with Noah, but I also felt there was now no going back. Tormented as I was, I had to discover the truth even if it was through the voice of another former enemy. Could Claypole help me find the person behind the attempted poisonings of such an unlikely trio as Rose Maylie, Mary Hogarth and Bill Sikes? And would the same person be the true murderer of Nancy?

12

The Sewer King

To those unfamiliar with London, it may come as a surprise to hear that not only can you earn your living in the sewers of our great metropolis but that many do. It is not so long ago that London's main sewers had their outlets on the riverside entirely open and anyone could enter and wander through them at will in any direction they chose. And they could explore them for many miles, providing they could cope with the stench that assaulted their senses at every step. Searching the sewers for lost items of property was deemed a good way of making a living but, at the time about which I am writing, a particularly dangerous one because it was not uncommon, especially at spring tides, for the river water to pour through the sewers in a raging torrent, drowning all in its path and then bursting up through the gratings in the streets. I have heard some say that when this happens certain sections of the city look like a Dutch town so intersected is London by flowing water. But I have not been to Holland to know if that's a true comparison.

In recent years the Metropolitan Commissioners have taken measures to control the water flow and restrict access to the sewers. They have bricked in most of the sewer entrances, leaving only strong iron doors as the means of entrance and exit. These doors are so hinged that they will swing open to let the sewer disgorge its contents but yet will stay closed against the pressure of rising river water. Sadly this has not stopped the poor visiting the sewers. It has only made it more dangerous for them as they search for the offscourings of the city. This is a profitable activity because there is always a great quantity of things being washed down from the cesspools and drains of the city's houses. When in luck, those searching the sewers may find items of expensive cutlery, articles of jewellery, valuable cups and plates, and, of course, coins, ranging from tiny coppers to silver sovereigns.

Those who make their living by what they discover within the sewers are known as 'toshers'. These men can still be seen along the banks of the Thames if you want to see them for yourself. They are easy to spot because most dress in long greasy velveteen coats, furnished with pockets of vast capacity, and they encase their nether limbs in dirty canvas trousers and wear any old slops of shoes for wading through the filth. Each carries a bag on his back, and in his hand a pole seven or eight feet long, on one end of which there is a large iron hoe. With this they can not only rake about the mud searching for iron, copper, rope, and anything else of value, but also test underfoot to make sure that they will not sink into some quagmire. I am told their way of life is still a dangerous one because the slightest tap may bring down an avalanche of old bricks and earth in those sections of the sewers which have been rendered rotten by the continual flow of putrefying matter. A tosher carries a lantern strapped to his chest so that he can illuminate his way, but this does not always give sufficient warning of broken channels or of the large gatherings of fierce rats that inhabit this underworld and which may, in their desperation, attack him.

Noah Claypole had disguised his role as a police informer by becoming a tosher. He had been sufficiently successful in his career to be able to purchase a number of riverside properties and add the title of landlord to his curriculum vitae. The police had informed me that because of this Claypole was now known among certain sections of the lower orders by the nickname 'the Sewer King'.

Noah's wealth may have stemmed in part from searching the sewers because the toshers are among the richest workers of our city, but I suspected his real wealth had stemmed from the greater rewards that had come from his actions as an informer — a role in which I knew, from my own experience, he excelled. Either way 'Sewer King' seemed an apt name for a man whose mind was as filthy and corrupted as any of the channels through which the city's rubbish flowed. Given our earlier history, I remained loath to reacquaint myself with my former tormentor, but my search for the truth gave me no option.

Claypole's home proved to be in a court off Rosemary Lane, an area renowned for its squalor and poverty. I entered his domain not with any pleasure but with understandable trepidation, and the weather matched my dismal mood. It was a dripping, comfortless day of almost incessant rain mingled with flakes of soot as big as snowflakes. The gloom of the dark clouds was equalled only by London's smoke, obliterating not only the sun but even the sky itself. Access to the court off Rosemary Lane was through a dark, narrow entrance, scarcely wider than a doorway, running beneath the first floor of one of the houses of the adjoining street. The court itself was about fifty yards long and not more than three yards wide, surrounded by lofty wooden houses, with jutting abutments from many of the upper storeys which almost excluded the light, and gave them the appearance of being about to tumble down upon the heads of any intruders. From many of the windows hung wooden rods on which tattered clothes hung, waiting for the rain to stop in the hope that they would then start to dry even if this meant they then revealed more fully their patched, faded, and ragged condition.

The court was densely inhabited and I suspected that every room in the thirty or so houses that bordered the courtyard, had at least one or two families living in it. The police had informed me that Claypole had over a thousand people packed into his properties. Judging from what I saw and smelt I could well believe it. The heavy rain meant the court was awash in liquid filth oozing from an overfull cesspit and I dreaded to think what conditions the residents of its cellars endured. The people who lived there were uniformly miserable. Dirty-shirted and baggy-breeched, their faces showed all the signs of that premature ageing which is brought about by a combination of too little food and too much gin. Indeed, though it was early in the day, I had to step over the bodies of a few who were already so drunk that they lay incapacitated in the mire. I looked for directions to one who appeared more friendly, though he was cadaverous and withered, with a head sunk beneath his shoulders and a face pinched by the signs of starvation.

I entered the house to which he directed me and went up three flights of narrow stairs. They creaked and trembled at every footstep, and the surrounding walls were stained with damp and dirt. If Noah had become a king, his castle was no Camelot. I knocked at the door at the top of the stairs and a jaunty and familiar-sounding voice within bid me enter. I entered a room, which I suspected was larger and much better furnished than most in the surrounding buildings, though it was still a spartan environment. Its floor was bare boards apart from one large rug, its walls were largely undecorated except by the stains of time, and its ceiling was unplastered, revealing the flooring of the room above. However, a large fire gave the room not only a welcome warmth but a glowing colour and the flue of the chimney, which was decorated with some heraldic carvings, stood out like a blackened buttress. Such furniture as there was in the room was heavy and well made.

The man sitting by the fire was dressed in

far more respectable attire than any I had met outside. He wore a shirt with an unusually large collar, dark corduroy trousers, and a light grey coat of a modern cut and decorated with bright brass buttons. It was unmistakably Noah. Although he had aged, the red nose, the mean mouth, and the small eyes set below an unusually large forehead were as distinctive as they had always been. So too was the rather petulant and audacious manner with which he stared at me. Not for the first time since I had begun my investigations I seemed to step back a dozen years. The first time we had met was when I had opened the door to him at Sowerberry's and he had taken an instant pleasure in tormenting me. This had become progressively worse when old Sowerberry began to use me as a mute in the funeral processions. With the benefit of years I understood Noah's motives in persecuting me. They were driven partly by jealousy and partly by the fact that, having been bullied as a charity boy himself, he delighted in bullying someone he perceived to be weaker than himself. Until, of course, the worm turned and I had thrashed him.

Noah interrupted my thoughts, saying, 'I'm so pleased to see you again after all these years, Oliver. It's been such a long time since we last met I can hardly recognize you. You're grown in height more than I expected when Charlotte and I fed you dog scraps at Sowerberry's and I've heard you've now become quite the gent. Certainly your clothes are very different from the rags you used to have to wear. No one would know you were once jist a workhouse brat or that you served time in a gang of thieves, pickpockets, and whores. Yes, Oliver, I have to say you look quite the young handsome dandy now. I'm honoured that you should ivver want to renew me acquaintance.'

Trying to keep my temper at his impertinent manner, I coolly responded, 'If it's all the same to you, Mr Claypole, I prefer we stick to more formal names. I know the police inspector has told you why I would like to see you, and I am grateful that you have agreed to a meeting. I am prepared to pay for what information you can provide, but there is no point in hypocritically pretending we were ever friends.'

The smile faded from his lips and Noah snarled in reply, 'Friends, maybe not, Mr Twist, but we seemed to spend our youth serving the same masters, first old Sowerberry and then Fagin. Don't talk of pretence to me when I know as well as you the company we kept and, in your case, some of the favours that were involved. Charlotte may have been a bit of a tart but at least my sexual tastes ran in normal channels. You were not the gentleman then, were you, Mr Twist?'

'As you well know, I became a member of Fagin's gang by force,' I replied angrily, 'But my memory is that you became one by choice. There is a difference. The abuse to which I was subjected was imposed upon me. You are well aware that I had no desire to become an object of Fagin's attentions.'

'And do you think there was no driving compulsion behind my actions? When poverty drives, needs must in my opinion,' muttered Noah. 'I expect you are surprised that I took up work in the sewers, but necessity drove me into it, just as it drove Fagin into theft and pimping. Only my choice was a wiser one, of course! Being a tosher has made me quite a success in this neighbourhood and it's been an interesting life. You can go a long way in the sewers if you like, although even I don't know how far. I nivver was at the end of them, for a cove can't stop in longer than six or seven hours, 'cause of the tide. You must be out before that's up.

'I can't say the work is exactly to my liking but there is always pleasure if, having put your arm to the shoulder in mud, you bring up something worth having. I often find spoons and knives and forks and bits of jewellery and I once even found a silver timepiece.

'Working in the sewers makes a man fit too. They say the smell drives away infection. It's a harsh smell at first, but nothink as bad as people thinks, 'cause, you see, there's sich lots of water always flowing through the sewer, and the air gets in from the gratings, and that helps to sweeten it a bit. I've heard tell there's some places, especially in the old sewers, where foul air can cause instantaneous death, but I nivver met with anythink of that kind.

'Mind you, if ever I come to a narrow place, I make sure I tek the candle out of the lantern and fasten it on the end of me pole and then I hold it ahead of me. If the light stays on, I know it's safe to proceed. The rats are a greater danger, but I go with three or four of me mates together, and the warmints are too clever to tackle us then, for they know they'd git off second best.'

'I didn't come to talk to you about the stinking sewers, Mr Claypole,' I interrupted.

'No, that's true. But perhaps you want some information about the sewage of society, Mr Twist.' Noah laughed at his own joke. 'Toshers could all be among the wealthier sections of society if they put their finds to proper use. As it is, most of 'em when they get a good haul spend the resulting money on drink. Large quantities of drink. And drink is a wonderful loosener of the tongue. It's amazing what you can overhear if you keep alert, especially as toshers mostly mix with the dregs of this great city. The police know I'm a very valuable source of information, Mr Twist. They respect me, and you'd do well to do the same if you want the information you seek. And respect means a little more politeness than I've so far seen and heard. And, of course, a clearer indication of the price you're prepared to pay. After all, a King is entitled to expect due homage and appropriate gifts.'

I will not bore you with the details but a deal was struck. I resented having to pay money to a man for whom I had no respect, but I had no choice, and, in fairness to Noah Claypole, he provided me with more information than I could possibly have expected. I will omit some of what he said but much I found so gripping I can almost repeat it verbatim.

13

Noah's Story

'As you know, Charlotte and me came to
London after there was a disagreement with
old Sowerberry over some money missing
from his till. For that reason we called
ourselves Mr and Mrs Bolter. I confess that
at that time I thought the easiest way to
become a gentleman was to help myself to
others' riches by making use of Charlotte's
undoubted talents in that direction. She
would do anything for me, would Charlotte.'

Noah gave a leer and winked at me
knowingly before resuming: 'We was discuss-
ing our future as thieves in a public house to
which we had been recommended when,
naïve fools that we were, we was overheard by
that damn Jew Fagin. As you have probably
guessed, the public house was, of course, the
Three Cripples, which members of his gang
often frequented. Fagin was quick to
introduce himself and to offer to gratify me
wishes. He told me I could live with him like
a gentleman — board and lodging, pipes and
spirits free — and keep half of what Charlotte

and I earned. It was an offer we couldn't refuse.

'Fagin was brilliant at identifying talent and he soon recognized mine was as a spy. I owe him a lot in that respect. The first task he give me was to go to the police station where the Artful Dodger had been taken prisoner. Poor old Jack had been unexpectedly stopped and searched and a stolen silver snuffbox found on him. Charley and his other mates could not understand how the Dodger had been arrested for so trivial a deed. The Dodger was not one to be taken like a common prig. Fagin disguised me in a wagoner's frock, velveteen breeches, leather leggings and a large felt hat. I was told to act the part of a country fellow from Covent Garden market, curious to see the workings of the city police. I became one of the crowds who gathered to listen to the Dodger's hearing 'fore the magistrate. Like all those present, I admired the courageous way he conducted himself. But every card was stacked agin him. He nivver had a chance. A man testified not only to the loss of the snuffbox but also to recognizing the Dodger as present in the crowd at the time of its theft. A policeman then testified to seeing him steal a handkerchief.

'When I reported all the case to Fagin and

how the Dodger had been duly committed to prison, he wasn't convinced that the arrest was all it seemed. As you know, Jack Dawkins was called the Artful Dodger 'cause of his immense talents as a thief. He was renowned for being able to avoid detection in his crimes, despite having the audacity to dress distinctively in a man's coat that reached nearly to his heels. Fagin told me he suspected the Dodger had been betrayed by Nancy and gave me the task of following her.

'Thus it was that I trailed the slut to her meeting with Mr Brownlow and Miss Maylie on London Bridge. I heard her laugh at the way she had given Bill Sikes laudanum so she could sneak out to see them. I heard them encourage her to betray Fagin and all his gang. And I heard her betray Monks. All this I told Fagin and he then took me to tell it all to Bill. That was not so much to me taste. I knew what the old Jew wanted. He wanted Bill to punish her. Punish her severely.

' 'Bill, suppose,' says Fagin, pointing to me, 'this lad was to peach — to blow upon us all. Suppose Bolter was to do it, of his own fancy — not grabbed, tried, imprisoned — but of his own fancy, to please his own taste; stealing out nights to do it, Bill. Suppose he did all this, what then?'

' 'What then? If he was left alive till I came,

204

I'd grind his skull under the iron heel of my boot into as many grains as there are hairs on his head.'

' 'What if I did it, Bill?' replies Fagin.

' 'I'd beat your brains out afore everyone. I'd smash your head as if a loaded wagon had gone over it.'

' 'And what if it was Nancy, Bill? Tell him about Nancy, Bolter. How you followed her.'

' 'You followed Nancy?' says Bill, staring at me as if he was about to kill me on the spot.

' 'Yes. To London Bridge where she met two people,' I says. 'A gentleman and a lady who asked her to give up her pals, and Monks first, which she did — and to describe him — which she did — and to tell her what house it was that we meet at, and go to, which she did — and where it could best be watched from, which she did — and what time people went there, which she did.'

' 'She told it all,' says Fagin. 'And tell Bill what they said about last Sunday.'

'They asked her why she didn't come last Sunday, as she promised. She said she couldn't because you, Bill, kept her forcibly at home. She said she had no laudanum to use on you as was her normal practice when she needed to be free of your attentions.'

'I got no further, for Bill was so enraged he made for to leave immediately to confront her. Fagin tried to hold him back, saying, 'Bill, you won't be too violent. I mean not too violent for safety. Be crafty, Bill and not too bold.'

'If murder was not on the Jew's agenda, Bill was too incensed to listen and he dashed out of the room, swearing and cursing, brushing both of us aside. Fagin ordered me to follow him. It was a bloody easy task. He was so furious with rage he cared not who followed him on his headlong course. He headed for his lodgings and I heard and watched all that happened after he had burst into his room. He grasped the unfortunate Nancy by the head and throat, dragged her into the middle of the room, and yelled her crime into her ears, calling her a she-devil.

'She pleaded for mercy and clung to him as he struck her again and again. She begged him to abandon his criminal way of life and get away from Fagin by accompanying her to some foreign country. In reply he took out his pistol and struck her a vicious blow across the forehead. Her blood poured on to the carpet, staining it bright red. As she pulled out a handkerchief to stem the flow, he struck her again.'

'Stop it! Stop it! I can't bear it!' I sobbed.

'Can't you bear it, Mr Twist? It may surprise you but neither could I. And that is why, although you may not believe me, I intervened. Running into the room I leapt on to Bill's back and prevented further blows. Looking back it was a damn stupid thing to do because he could easily have felled me as he had felled her, but my action seemed to snap him out of his fury. All his anger drained away almost as rapidly as Nancy's blood was pouring from the deep gash on her brow.

'And then he wept. The great brute wept like a blubbing baby at what he had done. Begged her forgiveness. Blessed me for stopping him. Said he'd nivver intended to harm her as much as he had. Together we stanched her wounds and carried her to the bed. Despite the obvious pain she was in, Nancy offered no curses. She simply looked at him with such love in her eyes. And she readily forgave him, telling him he deserved a full explanation of her actions.

'Battered though she was, Nancy indicated to Bill that she wanted me gone before she spoke, and he told me to get out. I instantly obeyed but I did not go far. Sikes was too agitated to make sure that I really had left and Nancy was still too weakened from his attack to leave the bed. I placed my ear next to the closed door and thus was able to hear almost all their conversation whilst they were unaware of my continued presence. The information I heard from Nancy's lips I have told no one, but time has moved on and I don't much mind speaking out now, especially as the terms of our contract are so good. The police will tell you I believe in giving good value for money.'

'But why wait until now! I don't understand. Why?' I demanded, grasping his shoulders as if I could shake the truth out of him. He pushed me away and smiled contemptuously.

'At the time it was a different matter. Silence seemed the better course of action. I did not want whoever killed Nancy to know that I knew Bill was innocent of her death. It's called self-preservation, Mr Twist. For all I knew speaking out then might have ended in me becoming the next victim. Besides, have you forgotten the extent of the chaos among all us members of Fagin's gang? We sought to hide ourselves as best we could and most of the gang I've nivver seen since. Even that old cow Charlotte, who I thought was besotted with me, vanished. She was a pathetic creature but I had hoped to use her talents in various ways and at the time I regretted her disappearance from me life. You can turn a pretty penny if you know how to sell a woman as sexually obliging as Charlotte could be.'

Once again I was treated to Claypole's lascivious smile before he continued: 'As it happened, I was one of the first to be arrested. At first I tried to stay dumb, but when I heard the news of Bill's death, I decided to save my skin by becoming the chief witness against Fagin. It seemed safer to let the world continue to think Bill was Nancy's murderer. After all, my testimony could not bring him back to life.'

'So what did Nancy tell Sikes?' I interjected.

'Something which it gives me pleasure to tell you, Mr Twist. Nancy told Bill that you were her child, taken from her when she was little more than a child herself. She begged him to understand why she wanted you to have a different and better way of life from her own. She explained that she had been able to produce false evidence that you were the heir to the property of a family called the Leefords. She had enlisted the help of a writer called Charles Dickens to ensure your removal from Fagin's clutches by telling him he had fathered you. Funny, isn't it, that you may have a worse mother than you thought but a very famous father!'

'But that's impossible! I cannot be his son,' I interjected. 'He's far too young and, besides, I know he would never have wished to become her lover.'

'I can only tell you what she said. If I had proof, don't you think I might have tried me hand with seeing Mr Dickens before now. That story would be worth a penny or two if it could be proved.' Claypole laughed at my discomforture, and then resumed his narrative. 'Nancy went on to tell Sikes the attempted burglary had been a put-up job with the express aim of making Fagin believe you had been shot and killed. Dickens had guaranteed to her that Bill and anyone else involved in the burglary would not be captured. Unfortunately, their plan had almost gone fatally wrong. One of the servants sent to fire the gun that would drive away Bill had panicked and ended up actually hitting you. As she told Bill this, I could hear her sobbing even at the memory of how close you had come to death.

'Once she had recovered her composure, she told him how matters had then got beyond her control for reasons she didn't understand. First of all, Dickens, who until then had been her willing gull, had refused to play his next part in her plan. This was to betray a man called Monks to the police. She told Bill that Monks was really called Edward Leeford and it was he she had deceived into believing that you were his half-brother.

Nancy had been confident that his arrest would have resulted in your becoming rich.

'However, Nancy said she had far worse to deal with than Dickens's new-found awkwardness. She felt she had strong cause to believe that someone was attempting to poison her and her son. Nancy believed others had fallen victim instead to this unknown person's murderous attempts. She reminded Bill of his own illness and told how the young woman called Rose Maylie, who was looking after you, had also almost died.

'At first she had thought the poison had been directed at those who had been taken ill, but, after reflection, she had realized this was not the case. She had come to believe she was the intended victim. Her protective attitude towards her son had not gone unnoticed among Fagin's gang and she thought one of them must have been tailing her and was now acting against her. For weeks she had been keeping a constant watch on those around her.

'She told Bill it was her view that the attempted poisonings were the work of the Artful Dodger. In the short time you had been in Fagin's hands, Dawkins had become very physically attached to you, Mr Twist. She believed his jealous passion at your removal lay behind his attempted murder of both her, the instigator of your escape, and you.

'Frightened and unable to confide her fears in anyone, she had taken the only course open to her. First, she had acted as informer to the police to secure the arrest of the Dodger, planting enough evidence on him to ensure he would probably be transported abroad to a penal colony. Secondly, she had risked seeing Rose Maylie and Mr Brownlow on London Bridge so that she could betray Monks herself. However, she told Bill she had refused to provide information to either them or the police on Fagin or any other members of his gang. She begged Bill again to forgive her.

'Although I could only hear and not see, I believe Bill kissed her. At least that's what it sounded like to me. He told her he would go find Betsy to patch her up and that he would put matters right with Fagin. Hearing him move, I hurriedly hid. He left the room and headed off.

'I made my own way back towards the Three Cripples where I had arranged to meet Fagin at a later hour. Before he and I met, the news of Nancy's murder was being shouted around the whole neighbourhood. I can only surmise that Nancy got it wrong and that the man out to destroy her was not the Dodger. Weak from loss of blood, she must have fallen an easy victim to her murderer, who finished the beating that Bill had commenced.

'I can't help thinking, Mr Twist, that it must have come as a terrible shock to Bill to hear of her death and to realize that he was believed to be the killer. No wonder he did not flee but sought information to avenge her. Only the dreadful accident in which he hanged himself put paid to his investigations.'

When Claypole had finished, my head was reeling with the information he had provided. I thanked him — more graciously than I had expected — and even shook his hand. I have no recollection of my departure from his house or indeed of how I got myself home. My brain was in a complete whirl. Only gradually did the questions begin to shape in my mind and certain thoughts to dominate. Nancy had engaged the support of Dickens because she had told him I was his child. Was this another of her lies or was he truly my father? If so, was the Dodger really the mysterious poisoner? If he was, then it was possible that Dickens might be the murderer of my mother. The attempted poisoning of Nancy had struck not only Bill Sikes and Rose Maylie but also Mary Hogarth, Dickens's sister-in-law. He had told me he believed Nancy had killed Mary. Demented by her death, had he gone to see Nancy and, seeing her battered condition, made use of the opportunity to avenge his sister-in-law's cruel sufferings? If the Dodger was not the poisoner, then who was? And had this mysterious monster abandoned poison to savagely bludgeon my poor mother to death?

Amid the questions, one thing became certain. I had to see the great writer again and I knew the meeting would not be an easy one. Dickens had not told me all the truth on our first meeting. Would I be any more successful on a return visit in obtaining what he truly knew about Nancy's murder? And would he admit to being my father?

14

Dickens Again

Dickens agreed to meet me again but this time not at his house. I suspect he feared a scene. He therefore preferred to hold our meeting elsewhere and told me to make my way to the ruins of Rochester Castle, a place he associated with the happiest days of his childhood. Rochester was not a place I knew but, as I walked along its old High Street, I admired its many old houses and strange gables, and understood a little why Dickens held the place in such affection. When I reached the castle he was waiting for me at the foot of its ancient, ivy-covered walls and he was the first to speak.

'I have happy memories of this place which I oft frequented as a child. Of course the town has shrunk fearfully from the picture I retained in my head. I had entertained the idea that the High Street was at least as wide as Regent Street in London, but now I find it is little better than a lane. The public clock, which I supposed to be the finest in the world, now appears to be as moon-faced and weak a clock as I ever saw, and the town hall, which I thought a model for the palace of Aladdin, is in reality a rather mean brick heap. It was a relief to come here and find this castle at least unchanged. A man's life seems a brief little practical joke in comparison with the solidity, stature, and strength of its walls, even though the blue sky now provides its sole roof and crows and jackdaws are its only warders.'

I made no comment and he went on. 'While waiting for you I climbed its rugged staircase, stopping now and then to capture glimpses of the Medway or to peer down through the gaps between the bare joists that are all that remain of former floors. The view from the castle ramparts on to the cathedral and the crumbling remains of the old priory is delightful. You can see the row of staid old red-brick houses where the Cathedral dignitaries live and the shrunken fragments of one of the old city gates. And the old trees with their high tops below me are just as I remember them. Oh, how I used to love this place when I was a child and I could dream its former glories back into life in my imagination! Don't you agree, Mr Twist, that there are few things in this beautiful country of England more picturesque to the eye, and agreeable to the fancy, than an old cathedral town. Have you been inside the cathedral?'

'No, not yet,' I replied.

'You must, if only to see the battered effigies of clergy long since deceased and the praying figures of knights and ladies on the tombs, with little headless generations of sons and daughters kneeling around them. And there is nothing quite like the soft and mellow light provided by cathedral stained-glass windows. It's no surprise to me that men and women believe their prayers may be better answered within such hallowed surroundings.'

'And both you and I may be much in need of prayer after this meeting,' I interrupted, sensing that his conversation was but a thin disguise to hide his nervousness at our second meeting.

He smiled and replied, 'I see you are keen to tell me what you have uncovered, so proceed, and maybe we will leave our sight-seeing till later.'

We moved to sit on a bench and there, under the leafy boughs of a tree, I outlined to him all the things that had happened to me since we had last met. Only a few passing birds bore witness to our meeting. He listened patiently but with increasing agitation, nodding his head and interrupting my story with the occasional phrase, such as 'God bless my soul,' or 'Oh Lord no!' He then asked me to wait while he walked for a time to compose himself.

I watched him pace backwards and forwards. He appeared deep in conversation with himself. Every emotion known to man seemed to cross his troubled face. At least a half hour must have passed by. Then he returned to tell me what was either the truth or a cleverly constructed story. How can you tell the difference when you are dealing with Britain's greatest storyteller? All I can say is that throughout our conversation he seemed to be one who could not stand still, but must be moving and that he waved his arms so dramatically it was a wonder his manner did not draw an audience and so negate the secrecy of our meeting.

'Last time we met I told you how it was Nancy who seduced me when I was still a child. And that was true,' he began. 'What I did not say is that, corrupted though she was, she was only a month or two older than I. She told me long afterwards that she failed to take any precautions. Whether that was because she thought me too young to be a danger to her or whether simply she was too drunk, I cannot say. She told me she became pregnant but was too frightened to tell anyone. Young in years though she was, she had seen the result of enough bloody backroom abortions for the prospect of one to fill her with terror.

'Inevitably a day came when her pregnancy could no longer be concealed. Of course, by then it was too late for her to have an abortion. She told me Fagin was furious and beat her most cruelly, almost to the extent where both she and the child were lost. However, he did not cast her out as she had expected. Apparently there is a market even for pregnant girls and Fagin always put cash first. It is hard to conceive — if you'll pardon that expression — of a more monstrous situation than a pregnant thirteen-year-old girl forced to engage in further sexual practices with deviant men, but that was Nancy's fate until she gave birth. She told me Fagin had planned it so that no one would aid her when the time arrived, but the other prostitutes intervened. It was fortunate that they did because the birth proved difficult and, had a midwife not been called, both mother and child would have been lost. As it was, Nancy suffered such damage that any future pregnancy became an impossibility. For that mercy she expressed her gratitude to God.

She was not allowed to keep the child for long. Fagin disposed of it. For nine years she pushed the memory of her unwanted child to the back of her mind knowing no one would wish to have a whore and a thief for a mother. Imagine her consternation when she saw the naked back of Fagin's latest recruit and recognized the one feature of her child she recalled with ease: a birthmark. Her instant response was to protect you and to that end she devoted all her energies. Her plan to palm you off as Leeford's stepbrother was inspired, but she needed an ally, and naturally she looked to the one other person who could be counted upon to help. That person was the father of her son. Our meeting in Newgate prison was no accident. What a fool I was. Nancy had been seeking me out for days.

'Nancy did not, at first, tell me of my own connection with you. As I told you before, I was on the lookout for a good story and she simply seized her moment to provide me with one. Telling me I was your father came later when she had to seek a means of ensuring I became not just a listener but also a participant in your rescue. Of course at first I refused to believe her, but Nancy arranged for me to catch a glimpse of you. That was all it took. You were the very spit of myself as a child. Look into a mirror, Oliver, and compare your features with mine.' He pulled out a small mirror from his coat pocket. 'Is the likeness still not apparent?'

It was true. As I looked at his marred but

still handsome face, I saw myself as I might look in the future.

'So you were prepared to not only betray my mother, but to abandon your own son!' I angrily shouted. 'Presumably a bastard son was an embarrassment to an author trying to make his name.'

'Yes, you would have been an embarrassment, although I was more concerned about how my wife would react than the reading public. But I did not desert you. Although I remained filled with hate for your mother, you were still my son, my innocent son. Don't you see, Oliver? My book on your life stuck to the lie she had created. If that was wrong, I am truly sorry. I did it for your own good.'

'But it suited you too. It removed any link between you and me. It convicted Bill Sikes of Nancy's death. If I were to be cynical, what better way to hide a murder than to convict another of the crime?'

'No, Oliver, believe me, I thought Sikes had killed Nancy. I will not disguise the fact that I revelled in the fact he had or that I wished I had had the courage to strike her myself. But you were my son. I did not abandon you. Nancy thought she had transformed you into a child with great expectations, but, in reality, she had not. It was a great blow to Mr Brownlow, who had become inordinately fond of you, when he discovered that poor Edward Leeford had squandered virtually all the family wealth and that your half of the inheritance was essentially one of debts.'

'That is why I am forever grateful for the way Mr Brownlow more or less adopted me and made me his heir.'

'So you see him as your benefactor?'

I nodded my assent. 'He was the kindest, most generous of guardians and he left me better placed financially than my mother could have possibly dreamed.'

'I do not question his kindness,' said Dickens, 'but you are looking at your real benefactor. I am afraid I lied to you at our last meeting. You were right in thinking that Mr Brownlow had no fortune of any note until recently. I denied knowledge of whence that money came but in fact I know its source. It was my newly found wealth as a successful novelist that funded your education and it is my money which today still sustains your current way of life. This may sound like the stuff of which novels are made, but ask your lawyer if you do not believe me. I will remove the gag of secrecy I imposed upon him. I am the man who has fulfilled the great expectations your mother wanted for you, not Mr Brownlow. He acceded to my offer of help because he knew you would benefit and he wrongly assumed that my generosity was simply a product of my thankfulness at the boost my career had received from writing your story. All I asked of him in return was that he should not disclose what I had done. Though reluctant to take the credit for himself, he let your best interests determine his response.'

My mind reeled at this latest revelation. My whole world appeared to have been built on lies and misunderstandings. I had been surrounded by deceit from the moment of my birth. And yet, looking at Dickens's earnest face, I did not doubt that he was telling the truth or that he needed me to respond to him as a son rather than as a stranger. But, as yet, I could not give him what he most wanted. My mother's death divided us. He was far too intelligent not to recognize that. Both of us grappled with our emotions and suppressed them. He reached out his hand and tentatively placed it on my shoulder. I managed not to recoil but I could not prevent some of my hurt finding expression.

'Has a child not the right to know who its parents are? My mother seems to have thought it was better for her child to believe Agnes Fleming was his mother than a common whore and thief. Maybe I can just about understand that. But you? Why should you also deny me? You obviously thought it was better for me to remain deceived, not only on this matter but also on the very source of my inheritance, rather than to know who my father was. Is that really fair? I can see it suited your reputation to keep our relationship secret. However, although I cannot speak for all children, I believe most would want to know their true parentage. Could neither of you see that it is more important to me to be wanted than to have money and possessions? How can I feel wanted when you have both denied me? And how can I now make any response to the father who, for all I know, might have murdered my mother?'

'Believe me, Oliver, I did not murder Nancy. My crime was only to betray your mother, but it was in the belief that she had destroyed one of life's angels. I hope you can find it in your heart to forgive me. I confess I cannot understand why I took the illnesses of both Sikes and Rose Maylie at face value. I must have been blind. Your information that these were also instances of poisoning means I have to accept that Nancy was almost certainly not Mary Hogarth's murderer. And, if that is the case, I have three overwhelming reasons to help you discover the real truth of what happened. I owe it to Mary. I owe it to your mother. And I owe it to my son because, if this mystery remains, I fear you may always suspect me.'

'Those are fine words, but I cannot see what more we can do. Who else is left to shed any light on these tragic events?'

Dickens looked across at me. 'There are two', he said, 'and their names are Charley Bates and Jack Dawkins. You and I will have to discover their whereabouts. The last I heard Bates had resolved to turn his back on a life of crime and he was a carrier's lad in Northamptonshire. As for Dawkins, although he was sentenced to transportation, he must still be traceable. If we put our minds to it, we may be able to find at least one of them.'

I found myself agreeing. What else could I do?

15

Fresh Revelations

It took some weeks and the help of Harry Maylie's police connections to discover that Charley Bates had ceased being a carrier's lad and had last been seen working as a travelling street-entertainer in the Midlands. Both Harry and Dickens were keen to accompany me, but I insisted on going alone in search of him. I left Dickens still relentlessly pursuing with all his journalistic skills what had happened to the Artful Dodger.

I cannot recall much of my long journey. My mind was not on the scenery through which I travelled, but I know I passed through many soot-covered towns, whose inhabitants lived out their servitude in an almost perpetual darkness. Through the industrialized areas through which I passed visitors sought in vain for any quiet and attractive scenery. All around were furnaces and factories, belching forth their fumes and flames. In overcrowded tenements and disease-ridden streets human misery was far more evident than human happiness. I prayed

226

repeatedly that my efforts would be rewarded and that I would find Charley Bates, but sometimes my mood was as black as the smoke-filled sky outside and I despaired. Even if I found him, would he really know any more about the sordid events that surrounded Nancy's murder than I had already discovered? And, if he did, would he be prepared to tell the person who had helped destroy Fagin's gang? I oscillated between moments of hope that the truth would finally be revealed and periods of deep despondency.

I first heard definite news that I was catching up with Bates at a small market town called Bakewell in Derbyshire. Having discovered that he had been entertaining crowds there only the previous day, I determined to set off early the next day for Cromford, which I was told was his next destination. That evening I ate well on cold veal pie and a gooseberry tart, reflecting all the while on my forthcoming conversation.

The next day I rose early. It was a gloomy morning and all the surrounding hills were covered with mist, but I was eager to be on my way. After I had walked a few miles the mists dispersed and for a time I enjoyed the beautiful scenery around me, furnished as it is with steep rocks and ancient woodland.

However, even here the hand of man had wrought destruction, for I saw the remains of many oaks, hollies, and mountain ashes which had been felled and stripped of their bark. As I passed through the villages of Winster and Wensley the weather once more rapidly deteriorated. Matlock Vale, which I had been assured was a wonderful sight, was obscured by heavy rain clouds, and I was glad to arrive just after noon at Cromford. On my entry to the town I was very conscious of the fact that Cromford's once rural cottages were now dominated by industrial buildings and that these, to use a phrase coined by Blake, were indeed dark satanic mills. Even the town's stream neither rippled nor cascaded because it was channelled by the hand of man to serve the needs of the cotton works.

I decided I had time to take a stroll to Arkwright's great mill, which had a reputation for looking after its workers more than most other factories, but I cannot say I envied them the conditions in which they lived and worked. The workers I saw looked exhausted and were filthy and unkempt. They smelt of oil and their clothes were covered with dust and grime and wispy trails of cotton fibre. When I briefly toured part of the mill I felt as if I was suffocating because the air I breathed was thick with cotton flue. I watched with horror young children — some, like me, products of the workhouse — crouching low beneath the noisy machinery, risking life and limb to gather waste and keep the threads functioning. I knew they faced severe injury and possible death if even just their hair or part of their meagre clothing got momentarily caught. And for the factory child there was no time for play because carding engines, drawing frames, and winding rovers never stop operating. The visit did little to raise my sinking spirits. It seemed to me that the mills were just another way in which society showed how it viewed children as entirely expendable. How can this country describe itself as Christian? Did not our Lord say any man mistreating children would be putting a millstone round his neck when it came to seeking salvation?

In sombre mood I took up residence at an inn called the Black Dog. It was no better and no worse than countless others I had stayed in on my journey, though its landlord, fat, stupid, and splay-footed, was more helpful than most. At some stage it had probably enjoyed a picturesque view but, as I looked from its begrimed windows, the inclement weather deprived the scenery around not only of any colour but also of the little beauty which had survived the area's industrialization. Even the crude clamour of the mill, so successful in blocking out the sound of any trilling bird, failed to cover the sound of the icy rain, which beat against the inn's windowpanes. Storm clouds scudded across the darkening sky, bringing more rain from the chill North Sea, and for a time the relentless downpour glazed the stone pavements, giving them the illusion of polished marble.

I waited till the worst of the weather was over before stepping outside again. Even so I had to pass through many a puddle and my feet were soon wet through. It was a busy market day that afternoon and the streets were crowded with impudent mechanics. They seemed heedless of the rain which had soaked their dirty heads and seeped into their drab clothes. Far from dampening their spirits, the rain appeared to have strengthened their resolve to amuse themselves at the expense of many a shopkeeper or stallholder. I passed many men standing in groups, smoking and gossiping, while around them street-sellers vied with the dirt-encrusted shops to sell anything and everything, from pocket combs and clothes'-pegs to guinea pigs and ferrets. Poor linnets, blinded in the vain hope that this would make them sing

more sweetly, vied for space with the skins of strayed and stolen cats, which had been flayed alive in order to get a better-priced pelt. Shrunken fruit, plumped out to look better than it was, competed for purchase with dried fish, hung from hooks and looking like bats asleep. Harassed women hurried to purchase what meagre items they could afford for their families and the air was filled with the din and confusion of countless loud voices simultaneously bellowing as they extolled the virtues of buying their produce or the rags that frequently passed for clothing.

A sickly-looking boy of about five or six years almost knocked me over as he ran home with some cheap scraps he had been given. The holes in his clothes at his elbows and knees revealed fearful sores and gashes. His naked feet were blue with the cold. His blond hair, still flattened by the earlier rain, was unbelievably dirty, and his face covered with a grime which even the heavy downpour had failed to cleanse. And yet his face bore traces of a beauty that, had the circumstance of his life been different, would have brought him much attention and won over many a female heart. He was wide of brow, firm of jaw, and had a pleasing line to his nose. It was the pinched mouth and the hardness around the eyes that spoke of experiences beyond his

tender years, while the signs of malnutrition gave his features an unpleasant hardness. I pressed some coins into his pitiful hand and asked if he could tell me where a street entertainer would be most likely to perform his act. After a moment's hesitation he pointed out where I should go, calling God's blessing on my head.

I quickly worked my way through the crowd. Bates was indeed where I had been told I might find him and his act had drawn quite a reasonably sized audience. The ready and businesslike way he conducted his buffoonery was quite remarkable and far better than I had expected to witness. Part of his act consisted in imitating the mannerisms of passersby. He seemed able to seize on their peculiarities and mimic them with just the right amount of exaggeration to make each a source of amusement. The pompous and the proud, the timid and the bold, the rich and the poor, all fell victim to his wicked gift. And he interspersed his routines with a humorous patter which made even the oldest joke seem wondrously fresh and amusing. It was obvious that the crowd liked him and their appreciation at the end of his act was expressed in tangible form as coins were thrown into his dingy hat.

As people dispersed I walked up to him.

Gone was the boy I remembered. On closer inspection, I saw the greasepaint with which he had smeared his face in a vain attempt to disguise the fact that his eyes were sunken and his face scored with the lines and wrinkles that stemmed from premature ageing. His cheeks were hollow and livid and I sensed that, beneath his showmanship, his frame trembled. He jovially extended his arm so I could add my money to the collection but there was a melancholy man behind the outward smile. I placed the expected coin in his hand. 'Hallo, Charley. Remember me,' I said. After a momentary pause, the painted mask that was his face seemed to crack. 'Let me look at you. Oliver? Is it really you?' I nodded. He smiled and winked. 'My, you're the fine gentleman, now. It's good to know one of us Fagin lads made good. But then, you always were the lucky one.'

'That's not how I remember it, Charley.'

'Ah, well, perhaps not. You were more sensitive than the rest of us. I thought picking pockets was the most daring thing a boy could do and I laughed at those who thought my life to be bad, especially those do-gooders who handed out religious tracts. I used to use them to light the occasional pipe. They seemed to forget that most of us lads couldn't read or write, and those of us who could knew tracts would nivver fill our bellies. They said we had lost our innocence. I think I may have been innocent once but boys don't stay innocent for long, do they, when they've no home of their own and it's a choice between starvation and theft?'

'It wasn't just theft we were expected to do.'

'Ay, that's true. It was an ill day when I began working for Fagin, who expected other services from us as well. You did well to get out of it.'

'Come, let me buy you a drink, Charley. For old times' sake,' I replied.

As we drank our beers in the nearby pub Charley told me something of his history following Fagin's capture. Frightened at seeing the evil Jew's execution, he had abandoned his illegal lifestyle and tried to settle to a conventional job, but he told me he soon appreciated that his talents were wasted as a carrier and that living in one place was not for him. I tried to hide my impatience. It was not his history that interested me.

'Couldn't settle, you see, Oliver. I've nivver been used to a proper home and it didn't come easy to start one. I didn't want to return to the thieving, tempting though that was, so I decided to put to a different use all that training Fagin had given me. As a pickpocket you learn to watch people very closely and both the Dodger and I used sometimes to amuse ourselves at night by imitating those we had robbed during the day. I found I could use that mimicry to earn my bread. And, if the audience gets bored, I use other means to amuse them. All that picking of pockets means I can do almost anything with my hands. I started with card tricks. All card tricks are just quickness of hand. The greatest art is what is called forcing, where you make someone take the card you wish 'em to and he's not conscious of it, but I particularly enjoy slipping the card like this.'

He took out a pack and showed me the ace of hearts. He then shuffled and reshuffled the cards, each time managing to place the ace wherever I requested in the pack, top, bottom, or centre. Seeing my amusement, he offered to do his sovereign trick if I would entrust him with one. I willingly agreed and placed one in his hand, which he then clenched. When he opened his fist the sovereign had been replaced by a farthing. He then stretched out his other hand and effortlessly drew out my pocket-handkerchief. To my surprise it had a knot in it. He told me to untie it. I did so and uncovered my original sovereign.

Charley laughed at my discomforture. I surrendered my sovereign to him.

'Do you want to see some more?' he said. 'I can take empty cups and make 'taters appear under 'em, or make a cabbage appear in your hat. Or I can show you some of my juggling with balls and knives and rings.'

I told him I'd prefer to just talk, if it was all right with him, and I ordered some more beers. He talked to me a bit about his early life before he had taken up with Fagin. He described how his father had killed his mother because she had sauced him for drinking too much. He had punched her so hard and so frequently that, after a few days of intense suffering, she had died. Fear that his young son might speak of what he had seen had led his father to throw Charley into the river in the hope that he would drown. Though rescued from that fate, the homeless child had soon been coerced into a life of crime. Once he had finished his own story, Charley listened with increasing interest as I told him about what I had uncovered. Of course my account was highly selective. I did not tell him I was Nancy's son or that Dickens was my father, but I told him of the poisoning attempts and Noah's account of the meeting between Nancy and Bill following the Dodger's arrest. I asked him whether she had been right to think the Dodger was out to destroy her.

'When you met us, Oliver, we appeared to you such a jolly crew. But think of what happened to you in the short time you were with us and then reflect what must have been our experience, living for years with that unholy sod, Fagin. We were taught all the best ways to steal and then he took pleasure in tormenting us with the constant prospect of the gallows. He found it amusing that we daily risked our lives. We were encouraged to spy on one another and made to feel it was good when he beat one of the others. It was fear more than fun that made us dance to his devil's tune. And as you know, we were subject to constant abuse because he expected us to engage in whatever sexual acts he wished for himself or his clients. If we clung to each other it was because it was the only home we knew, however much we hated and despised it.

'For years Fagin delighted in playing us off against one another, but when you arrived his power was definitely on the wane. The Dodger, although outwardly still subservient, was increasingly becoming his own man. Nancy, for so long his creature, was becoming openly defiant and no longer prepared to do all he asked. And Fagin felt increasingly powerless to cope with these challenges to his authority because of his fear of Bill. Even Toby Crackit felt able to increasingly be rude to him.

'Nancy was right in thinking that one of the gang was out to get her, Oliver, but, believe me, it wasn't the Artful Dodger. It was that foul filthy Jew. The poisonings were his first efforts to regain control over her. I was the vehicle he used. Recognizing your hold over her, he was confident that possessing you would mean he could once again control her. After the failed burglary he sent me out to where you had been captured, with instructions to find out whether you had really been shot. He told me that if I discovered you were alive I was to make sure you were not moved till he could arrange to get you again, and he gave me the means to achieve that. Rose Maylie innocently provided me with the information I wanted and I seized the moment to make her an easy target. I slipped enough poison into a glass of milk to ensure that she would be mightily ill. With the house's attention directed on her, there was every chance we could get at you.'

I found it hard to accept that Charley could talk of such matters so calmly, almost as if he had no responsibility for his actions, and he sensed my unspoken criticism.

'The mask I wear for my act, Oliver, is me. There is no Charley Bates, just a performer doing his tricks. Don't look to me for any signs of regret. I have no conscience because Fagin destroyed it. I have no feelings because I could not have survived as long as I have if I had kept them. I learnt always to do what Fagin wanted and, unlike Nancy, I did not question. When I returned, I told Fagin what I had done and I believe he went out with Monks to spy out the land, but he wanted Bill put out of the way first before we did anything else. Sikes knew too much, and his frequent taunting of Fagin had not galled the Jew any the less because the wounds were hidden. He gave me something to drop into Bill's drink, something stronger than what I'd given Rose Maylie. Unfortunately for Fagin the combination of Sikes's constitution and Nancy's nursing proved even more potent than the poison.

'Bill's illness only made matters worse because it was too obvious that Fagin had taken no steps to enable Bill to recover. When the Jew belatedly tried to act as his friend again, Bill told him to take his withered claw off his shoulder. He accused him of being a black-hearted bastard. Their partnership had never been a happy one, but it now had no basis on which to continue. All that remained was total mistrust and scarcely concealed animosity. Fagin became so desperate that he even dared approach Nancy herself and suggest that she should poison Bill, telling her he had the means close at hand. Her spirits were obviously low and the Jew dared to hope that she had tired of her brutal lover. He told her he alone was her staunch friend, whereas Bill treated her worse than his dog. He described Bill as just the hound of a day, but one who would maim and destroy anyone else whom Nancy loved. Fagin hoped thus to strike a double blow. He would eliminate Bill and his knowledge of Nancy's crime would ensure his ascendancy over her again. Of course she refused. Hence his decision to use Bolter to follow her. He was desperate to find some evidence that he could use to blackmail her and regain control.

'I also am pretty confident that Fagin was behind the arrest of Jack. He wanted to remove a boy who was becoming a man able to challenge him. Making sure the police discovered his whereabouts and ensuring stolen goods were on him at the time was an easy solution.'

'But what about Mary Hogarth's death?' I interrupted. 'Who was responsible for that?'

'I don't know. I nivver heard her name mentioned by anyone. Her death may have been due to some medical weakness rather than any outside force. Maybe it was God, if you dare believe in him, who killed her. If Dickens had not heard Nancy's threats and seen her converse with Mary, maybe he would never have suspected any foul play.' Bates paused, seemed to hesitate, and then, pulling me closer to him, whispered, 'If she was poisoned, have you thought it might have been your precious Dickens who did it? Maybe Nancy told Mary Hogarth things he did not want known about his past. Maybe he feared what his sister-in-law might tell his wife? Maybe he poisoned her before she could take any action?'

'No! That's impossible!' I declared. 'Dickens was distraught by her death. I have heard him speak of it and the anguish is still there for anyone to see.'

'I've heard tell he is a good actor as well as a writer,' replied Bates, 'but you may be right and he might be innocent.' He smiled at my obvious support for the great writer but, even as he did so, his features were twisted by a bout of coughing that shook his entire frame. He held a foul-looking cloth that served as a handkerchief to his mouth and I noted the red marks, which indicated it was not just phlegm that was flowing from his throat. At once I understood why Bates looked so prematurely old and, beneath the extrovert show of the performer, frail. Consumption was eating away at his lungs. I grasped his hand and he registered my concern with a grateful glance.

'You can see by my attire that I am a wealthy man, Charley,' I said. 'Accompany me back to London and I'll ensure you have the best medical help. If you continue as you are, then there will be only one outcome and that is an early grave.'

'I've done many bad things in my life, Oliver, but I've nivver had to step so low as to take charity from any man and I don't intend to start now. Besides, believe me, the disease is too far gone for any doctor to make a difference. And, if I'm honest, I don't regret that. I've had enough of being on the road. To tell the truth, I've had enough of life.'

Another bout of coughing racked his body. Once he had recovered and wiped away yet more traces of blood from his lips, Bates rested against the wall of the inn. He began twiddling with the buttons on his frayed coat and somehow I sensed he was debating whether to offer an alternative solution to my own problem. After a momentary hesitation, he looked up and muttered, 'I'd like to help you, Oliver. May be it's the last good deed I'll ever do. You see, I may be uneducated but I am no fool and I have seen enough crime to understand the various motives that may lie behind the actions of men and women. I can therefore suggest another set of circumstances, although you may not choose to accept it. Maybe, Oliver, there was more to Dickens's relationship with Mary Hogarth than his wife liked. I've nivver met the woman but it's amazing what any jealous woman will do, even to a beloved sister. I therefore suggest that maybe you need to speak further to Mrs Dickens about her sister's death.' He drew back and waited to see my response.

'Maybe I do,' I replied.

Little more was said between us. When I left, he remained behind to drink further and we parted friends. My last sight of his frail and sickened form was of him beginning to attract others to his table by commencing some of his card tricks. 'Let's be merry, lads,' I heard him say with a bitter laugh. 'There's nothing in life as good as a bit of fun!' The showman had returned but, I suspected, not for very long.

16

Mrs Dickens

I saw Mrs Dickens before I saw my father again. I did not even tell him that I was meeting her. She was not as I had expected her to be. Although her features were not beautiful, she was more attractive than some of Dickens's comments about her had led me to think. Though rather plump and not very tall, she had the fresh-coloured complexion and large, heavy-lidded blue eyes so often admired by men. Her nose was slightly turned up, but she had a fine forehead and a small, red-lipped mouth that gave a genial, smiling expression to her countenance. I could certainly see what had attracted him to her. She had a natural kindness to her manner and this despite the fact that she was evidently agitated at meeting me in secret. In her hand she held the note I had sent her and its crumpled state bore witness to her anxiety. I hesitated over what to say and so she was the first to speak.

'You say that we need to speak about the death of my sister before you speak to my husband. Would you like to explain yourself, Mr Twist, because to my knowledge you never met Mary and can know nothing about her tragic death?'

'You are correct, madam, in saying I never knew her, but I have reason to believe that her death was not all that it seemed.'

Her face visibly paled but she rapidly composed herself and replied, 'I do not know what you mean, sir, but I find your manner impertinent and I suggest that you leave.'

'And tell your husband instead?'

'Tell him what, sir?'

'That you poisoned your own sister,' I replied.

The gamble — and it was a gamble because I had no evidence whatsoever — paid off. She did not need to speak. The blood drained from her face and her guilt was all too evident. She saw the look of triumph in my eyes and sank into a chair, saying, 'How much do you want for your silence?'

'I am not a common blackmailer,' I snapped. 'Tell me the truth and I will judge whether I will speak to your husband or not.'

After a moment's hesitation, she commenced her sorry story:

'I was attracted to Charles the moment I first met him. At that time he was still seeking to make his name but his confidence had been deeply affected by the breaking up of a longstanding courtship with a young woman. I gathered that her parents had disapproved of Charles. They thought he was not good enough for their daughter. Given his fame and success now, they must bitterly regret that decision. When not working he was lonely and depressed and I comforted him. Our friendship grew naturally into love and my father, recognizing his prodigious talent, happily and speedily gave his consent to our marriage. We could only afford to set up home in small, three-roomed lodgings but it seemed like a paradise to me. No wife loved her husband more than I or felt more loved in return. I was overjoyed when I became pregnant with our first child, little realizing the problems that would ensue after his birth.

'After our son was born, I suffered from some inexplicable nervous debilitation. Although physically I recovered from the birth quite quickly, I was unable to nurse my baby and so, with great reluctance, had to suffer him to be tended by a stranger. Every time I looked at my child I would burst into floods of tears. I became convinced that he would never love me because I had failed to nurse him. My husband tried hard to be sympathetic but he was hard-pressed by his own concerns at the time, having undertaken many different commissions. In the end he borrowed money so that we could move away temporarily from London to the healthier air of Kent. It made no difference to me but it meant that he had constantly to travel to and from his work in London. It is not surprising that his feelings for me began to wane. A depressed wife is no pleasure to a husband.

'It was his need to write your story, Mr Twist, that brought us back to London, but not to our former love-nest. Charles rented a far larger house in Doughty Street, one large enough to accommodate servants to look after me. My younger sister, Mary, insisted on joining us to help me. I readily assented because Charles was working exceptionally hard and was frequently absent for hours on end. I foolishly thought that to have my sister with us would help our marriage. Little did I know that she was to prove the serpent in our already disintegrating garden of Eden. Unbeknown to me, Mary had fallen in love with Charles and was therefore deeply jealous of our love for each other.

'It pains me to say it but Mary began to make deliberate attempts to seduce my husband away from me. She was the beauty in the family, not me, and she was prepared to flaunt her superiority in ways that I found hard to counter. I was prettier then than I am now, but that is not saying a great deal. For a long time I was unaware of what was happening, but eventually I became increasingly suspicious. When Charles was at home he spent as much time with Mary as he did with me.

'As time passed I began to notice that he was spending more time with her than with me. I would enter the room and find the two of them deeply engrossed in talking to each other, but their conversation would then cease and Charles, although never Mary, would sometimes look guilty. Mary always managed to look and sound like an innocent angel. I had no one to confide in because I knew that no one would believe me. They would think my concerns were the imaginings of a sick and depraved mind, another expression of the nervous exhaustion that had affected me after my son's birth.

'Eventually I decided to wait until Charles was absent from the house and challenge Mary. I expected her to deny my allegations and accuse me of insane and unfounded jealousy. If she had, maybe I would have chosen to believe her. In a strange way that would have been less painful than having to admit that I was losing the affections of my husband.

'However, Mary chose not to deny what

248

was happening. On the contrary, she gloated over her achievement in making Charles love her. She told me in the greatest detail the extent to which he had confessed his undying passion for her and, although there had as yet been no physical expression of that, assured me it had not been from any lack of desire. She said she was far too clever to submit to his embraces and risk becoming a mistress of the moment, especially as she knew that part of her attraction for Charles was his mistaken view of her purity and innocence. She told me my constant state of nervous debility made me unfit to be his wife, and she made it clear to me that her sole object was so to arouse him that he would divorce me and marry her.

'I broke down. I pleaded with her. I got down on my knees and begged her to leave my marriage alone. She simply laughed in my face. My anguish turned to anger and I railed at her that I would send her immediately back to my father. She merely taunted me with the fact Charles would never permit it and, in my heart of hearts, I knew that to be true. I threatened to kill her rather than see my husband taken, but this only reduced her to further merriment. She said the only person who would die would be me. Die of shame that I had neither the looks nor the charm to retain a husband's affection.

'And then she said the cruellest thing of all. She said Charles had only married me on the rebound and that he bitterly regretted his precipitate action in taking me as his wife. It hurt me more than anything else, for I feared it might be true. Even on the day of our marriage, I knew that part of his heart still yearned for his first love.

'After our clash, things got worse. Outwardly Mary played the devoted sister whenever anyone else was present. When we were alone it was a different story. She gloated over me, telling me in every detail, real or imagined, what Charles was saying to her and how he sought her caresses. She said it would be only a matter of a few months at most before he gained the courage to desert me. I did ask Charles if it was not time for Mary to return home. I even dared suggest that some of the neighbours thought it unseemly for a husband to spend so much time with a beautiful seventeen-year-old girl. He refused to listen and accused me of listening to malicious gossip. I dared not challenge him with the truth of his actions for I feared that would only precipitate the crisis of his leaving me. Instead, I did the only thing Mary could not achieve. I made sure he made me pregnant again.

'When I gave the news to Mary, she was furious. She screamed at me incessantly for the rest of the day. When I told Charles I was pregnant he was at first taken aback. However, he loved children and the thought of having a second child of his own clearly pleased him. Over the next few days he was more attentive to me than he had been for weeks. Shortly afterwards, I became very ill. I kept being sick and I feared I would lose my baby. Charles thought it was just morning sickness and at first so did I. But then one day I entered the breakfast room early and noticed that Mary was placing some powder into my morning tea. I hastily left the room before she noticed my presence, my mind awhirl with what I had seen. I realized then that Mary was secretly poisoning me either in the hope of aborting my child or of removing me altogether.

'That evening we were due to attend the theatre and Mary went out to purchase some new gloves. I made use of the opportunity to search her room and I discovered the powder in one of her drawers. I took it, replacing it with some flour that looked not dissimilar. Believe me, Mr Twist, I was thinking more of my safety than wreaking any revenge when I took that poison. However, at the theatre Charles's play made me furious. It concerned a marriage in which the husband had clearly become bored with his wife. Here, see for yourself.'

She walked over to the bookcase and extracted a manuscript, which she passed to me. On opening it, I found that the script was entitled *Is She His Wife? or, Something Singular!* 'Read the opening lines and you'll see what I mean,' she said.

I did as she asked and began reading the text aloud. I now have a copy of it and so I can show you exactly what I read out:

Lovetown:	Another cup of tea, my dear? O Lord!
Mrs Lovetown:	I wish, Alfred, you would endeavour to assume a more cheerful appearance in your wife's society. If you are perpetually yawning and complaining of *ennui* a few months after marriage, what am I to suppose you'll become in a few years? It really is very odd of you.
Lovetown:	Not at all odd, my dear, not the least in the world; it would be a great deal odd if I were not.

She grasped the manuscript back and I could see the deeply etched grief in her face.

'Ostensibly, Mr Twist, this so-called character Lovetown has tired of his marriage because he has to live in the countryside rather than in London. I recognized what the audience did not. The speeches between Lovetown and his wife contained word for word some of the very things said between my husband and myself. When Mrs Lovetown says, 'I could bear anything but this neglect,' she is expressing my grief and pain. When Mr Lovetown declares, 'I could put up with anything rather than these constant altercations and little petty quarrels,' he is simply repeating what Charles had said to me on more than one occasion. In the play both husband and wife pretend to have an affair to arouse each other's jealousy and rekindle their passion, but I knew Charles's affair was real and not imagined. Mrs Lovetown tells her husband 'Alfred! Alfred! How little did I think when I married you that I should be exposed to such wretchedness!' Replace the word 'Alfred' with the word 'Charles' and again you have my very words. My husband was presenting the breaking up of our marriage to the general public. Imagine how I felt, Mr Twist!'

She thrust the manuscript back on to its

shelf with disgust etched on her face.

'And he was sharing our domestic tragedy not just with the public but also with Mary. Unlike me, she found the play most entertaining and immensely funny. All evening she kept looking at me and laughing at me. I left that theatre hating her in a way that I had never thought possible. Looking back I am still not clear what I hoped to achieve when, after we had returned from the theatre, I poured the powder into Mary's bedtime drink. I think I wanted merely to give her back some of her own medicine and make her as sick as she had made me. I think I only wanted to end the laughter that had cut me to the quick. But if part of me wanted to make her as sick in the stomach as she had made me sick at heart, I have to confess that part of me wanted to kill her. That is probably why I put as much of her poisonous powder into the cup as I dared.

'You know the outcome. Mary became desperately ill very quickly and died later the next day. I was stricken with remorse and her death led to consequences I had not foreseen. First, our mother collapsed with grief. Then my own guilt led my body to abort the very child I had hoped to save. Worst of all, Charles was totally distraught for weeks. He did not merely wallow in her loss, he nearly drowned in it. He insisted that nothing of hers should be thrown away. Even two years after her death I discovered him one night taking out her clothes so that he could caress them. He still carries around with him a lock of her hair and wears her ring on his finger as if she and not I were his wife. He has twice immortalized her in his novels, once as the character of Kate Nickleby and once as Little Nell. God help me, Mr Twist, but in her death Mary attained a perfection she never achieved in life.

'I knew Charles was convinced that Mary's death was not a natural one, but he was unable to prove it to anyone's satisfaction. Not even to the doctor who attended her death. Either the doctor was incompetent or else the poison Mary purchased was subtle enough in its consequences to avert his medical suspicions. The doctor put down her death to heart failure. Fortunately for me Charles got it into his head that the source of the poison was some sweets, which we had purchased from a street-seller outside the theatre. I am not sure what I would have done had he accused me, but maybe it would have been better if he had. Although I have been pregnant for most of the time we have been married, Charles has never been the same to me since Mary's death. He rarely takes me out, contrasting my lethargy with his energy, my slowness with his quickness, my low spirits with his love of life. On one occasion, impatient with the physical weakness my pregnancies have wrought, he pronounced this place was more like a hospital ward than a home. He might just as well have called it a prison.

'Now that you know how I came to murder my sister, Mr Twist, do with the information what you wish. I am already in hell so it will make little difference to me. There are too many times when I feel I have not kept my husband after all. Even in death, I believe Mary won.'

Mrs Dickens's account moved me deeply. I felt she was receiving enough punishment for her actions without me adding to it. I therefore promised her I would say nothing to her husband and I kept my word. When I saw Dickens I told him what Bates had told me about the poisoning of Rose and Bill Sikes. I said Bates thought Mary's death was natural and the result of no action by Nancy or any of Fagin's gang. My father kept his counsel but he is a very astute man and I suspect he may then have begun to entertain greater suspicions about his wife's role in Mary's death. With his journalistic experience, it would not have been difficult to put the pieces of the jigsaw together. Certainly I know their marriage deteriorated further after my visit and whatever remaining affection he had for her was totally lost. I suspect Catherine Dickens was more than punished for her actions in removing her rival.

17

The Artful Dodger

My investigations following the receipt of Fagin's letter had revealed far more than I had ever hoped possible. In the process they had reshaped my whole understanding of the events of my childhood. I had confirmed that I was not the missing heir of Edwin Leeford. His son had been my friend Dick, who had so tragically died in the workhouse. I was no love child but a bastard born from the effective rape of Charles Dickens by the whore Nancy when both of these were little more than children themselves. Torn from my mother's arms and consigned to a pauper's existence, chance alone had reunited me with my real mother. Once I had been enticed into Fagin's den only the birthmark on my back had saved me from a life of crime. Its uncovering had led to Nancy's rediscovering the child for whom she had long grieved. Her love for me had led to her challenging Fagin and all around her to ensure I did not stay in the gutters of London and end my life on a hangman's rope.

It was Nancy who had conceived the plan of passing me off as the child of Agnes Fleming and therefore Edwin Leeford's heir. In return for cash Mr and Mrs Bumble had proved willing accomplices in deceiving the naïve Edward Leeford, alias Monks, into believing that I rather than Dick was his half-brother. Mr Brownlow's imagination had helped because he had wrongly assumed I was the very image of Agnes Fleming, although he had never met her and only had a poor portrait on which to base his judgement. Enlisting the help of my father, Charles Dickens, they had arranged the bungled burglary that would ensure my freedom from Fagin and the publication of my story. Dickens had also become the source of my income, permitting me to think it was Mr Brownlow who was my benefactor.

And then matters had gone horribly wrong. Dickens's wife had poisoned her sister, Mary Hogarth, because she was seeking to have an affair with Charles, but he thought that the murderer was a jealous Nancy. Seeking revenge, Dickens had betrayed Nancy to the men he knew would wreak vengeance on her if they knew she was communicating with gentry. Fagin, determined to regain full control of his gang, had informed on Nancy's friend, the Artful Dodger, and ensured his arrest and subsequent transportation, but had sown the seed that the Dodger had been informed on by Nancy. He had then used Charley Bates to poison both Rose Maylie and Bill Sikes. The poisoning of Rose Maylie had simply been a ploy to enable my recapture. The poisoning of Bill Sikes was a more sinister attempt to eliminate Nancy's lover, who was the man Fagin most feared.

When Bill unexpectedly survived this attack, Fagin used Dickens's information to persuade him that Nancy had become a police informant. In this way he hoped to remove both of them forever. Noah Claypole had witnessed the outcome of Bill's fury at first hand. Though he had struck my mother, he had not killed her. The assumption that he was the murderer and his accidental death while fleeing the mob had permitted the real murderer of Nancy to escape justice.

However, all my investigations had brought me no nearer discovering who had murdered Nancy. It was my father, Dickens, who now took over the search for the truth, using all the many people he knew as well as his considerable skills. The one key figure we had not spoken to was Jack Dawkins, the Artful Dodger and it was just possible he might be able to shed light on who would have had cause to kill her.

Using his foreign connections, Dickens discovered that the Dodger had made the most of his opportunities when sentenced to transportation and had become a wealthy farmer with large estates to his name in Australia.

I was all set to embark on a journey across the world but that proved unnecessary. His informants told Dickens that Dawkins had returned to England under an assumed name. However, this made finding him appear an impossibility to both Dickens and me. It was Harry Maylie who tenaciously continued the effort to discover his whereabouts, instituting as many inquiries as he could through the network of police informants. I suspect Rose was behind Harry's determination to finally solve the mystery of Nancy's murder. She had always felt a degree of guilt at her and Brownlow's failure to protect her.

A few months after my meeting with Mrs Dickens Harry arrived, hot and breathless at my house, clutching a letter addressed to me. It had been handed into his office while he was out. The person who had left it had told Harry's clerk to tell him it was from the Dodger. The clerk's description of the man was not particularly good. Harry said he could recall only that the man was fashionably dressed, that he was bow-legged and small in stature, and that his face contained a rather snub nose and small eyes. However, this was sufficiently close to my memory of the Dodger to excite me and I eagerly opened the envelope. Inside was the following short message written in an untidy scrawl:

I thought I had put behind me the days when I was known as the Artful Dodger, so it came as something of a shock to discover so many people suddenly seeking to find me. Your friends in high places are persistent buggers and I fear it is only a matter of time before they discover my identity, so I am asking you to call them off. Returned convicts, however reformed, are not welcome back and you know the penalty I will face if I am caught. I have no desire to end my life on a hangman's rope. I don't know the reason for you seeking me, but, for old times sake and the good of my neck, I am prepared to meet you at midnight on London Bridge. Come alone and unarmed or, believe me, you will never see or hear from me again.

Harry tried to dissuade me from going alone, but I refused to listen. I had come too far to turn my back on what might be my last chance of resolving my mother's murder.

When I left my home the weather was not auspicious. It was a dark night, and bitter cold. The bleak east wind brought with it stinging particles from marsh and moor and fen. As the church clocks chimed, I stood near the centre of the bridge. At that hour and place there were few people around and those hurried past me in the mist, keen not to get too close to a stranger. It was so quiet I could hear the rippling of the water against the barges. The river was swollen and the tide was running down very strong. The natural gloom of night made not only the air black but the water black and the surrounding buildings black. It was virtually impossible to see the jumble of old smoke-stained warehouses on either bank, let alone the dense mass of roofs and gables beyond them. The shadows were only a deeper shade of black amid the blackness. Only the tower of old Saint Saviour's church and the spire of Saint Magnus were visible above the mist.

The sight reminded me of what Dickens had written all those years ago. I was standing on the very spot where Nancy had met Mr Brownlow and Rose Maylie and I suspected the Dodger's choice of venue was not accidental. I stared at the sluggishly flowing water and my imagination summoned strange and fantastic forms from the dark shadows.

The rushing water seemed to convey the sounds of gurgling and drowning and the occasional dip of oars and their rattling in the rullocks from some passing boat sounded like the ghostly rattlings of iron chains. My foolish fancy took flight and I sensed that I was being watched by water rats of human growth and that they were waiting for the crushing blow to my skull that would send me tumbling unconscious into their midst.

A voice in my ear interrupted these ridiculous reflections and summoned me to follow it. I turned and a small figure dressed in black emerged from the mist, beckoning towards some steps that led downwards. I followed as directed and found myself going down two flights of stairs. The stone wall on my left ended in an ornamental pilaster facing towards the Thames. Standing with his back to it was my guide. In one hand he held a gun. With the other he pulled away from his head the scarf that concealed his features. It was indeed Jack Dawkins. The snub nose, flat brow and sharp, ugly-looking eyes were unchanged, although his hair was grizzled and his face lined more than I had expected for someone scarce older than me. He looked an old man.

His had been the first face I had come to know when I had fled to London, a frightened and lonely boy of nine. And he had rescued me with an offer of friendship. I recalled how easily he had deceived me and how much he had entertained me on that first long journey to Fagin's lair. We had crossed from the Angel Islington into St John's Street, and then headed down Rosebery Avenue, which is marked at its beginning by Sadler's Wells. We next moved through Exmouth Street and Coppice Row towards Saffron Hill. And all along the streets had got narrower and muddier and the air more foul and putrid.

But nothing had tamed his high spirits. He had kept me entertained with a constant round of stories and with witty comments made about the places and people we passed. Covered ways and yards, which here and there diverged from the main street, disclosed drunken men and women wallowing in filth, and these hopeless souls had become the object of much of his clever mirth. The sight of great, ill-looking fellows emerging from some public houses had ensured that I clung still more tightly to his company till we reached the bottom of the hill and he pushed me through the doorway of the house near Field Lane, where my education was to truly begin.

But the light-hearted boy in the ill-fitting

clothes, which reached nearly to his heels, and the large hat which threatened to fall off every moment, was gone. Before me was the hardened face of a criminal whose life had moved beyond the amusement of youth to the cynicism of adulthood. His eyes stared with a fierceness that recalled Bill Sikes rather than the Dodger. His mouth was hard and his lips turned back in a scowl that made me tremble. There was no hint of friendliness and clearly deep resentment at having to meet me again. But who could blame him? Now he saw me as his persecutor and, looking at the anger and bitterness of his gaze, I am not ashamed to say that I feared his would be the last face I would see before he ended my days. The river is a great consumer of bodies and I knew mine could easily become just one more swollen and disfigured mass in its watery embrace.

'If I had known what your arrival would cause to happen to Fagin and the rest of us, Oliver, I'd nivver have spoken to you the first time we met.'

'Please believe me, Jack, when I say I had no wish to harm any of you then and I've no wish to harm you now. The past is the past and, if you have made a new life for yourself, I am pleased for you.'

He smiled and laughed. It was the same

sound I remembered so well from when he and Charley engaged in their games. 'My God, you're still the damn little prig you ever were, Oliver. I can only hope the outcome of our second meeting will be a happier one, but you'll understand my caution. Fagin taught us to search each other well, Oliver. You won't mind if I frisk you.' I nodded my assent. He grasped me by the shoulder and made me spread-eagle myself against the wall. I felt as if I was being stalled up — a phrase pickpockets use when they are setting up a man to be frisked and rifled. Finding me to be unarmed, he visibly relaxed and gestured to indicate that I should sit down on the dank steps. I obeyed and he then settled himself by my side so that there was no chance our whispered conversation being overheard.

'Ay, Oliver,' he confided, 'things have changed since we last met. I've made a new life for myself. The crossing to Australia in what was little better than a coffin ship introduced me to some experiences I'd rather forget. There were about thirty of us lads on board and we were kept in the same conditions as the men. Some of the convicts targeted one or two of us for their sexual gratification, even going so far as to give them female names. I felt fortunate that I was an ugly sod. The crew did nothing to protect us but whipping convicts for other activities was almost the only source of amusement to some of the sailors. The cats they used were each six feet long, made out of the log-line of a ship of five hundred tons' burden. Nine over-end knots were in each tail and the nine tails whipped at each end with wax-end. With this they gave half-minute lashes because a quicker lashing would have resulted in certain death. Some of my fellow convicts appeared immune to its punishment. I saw one rub his shredded back against the mast till he squeezed congealed blood out of it just to show his contempt. He was given a further twenty-five lashes for that.

'My turn for punishment eventually came — I had the misfortune to drop a bag of flour I had been asked to take to the cook. None of my dodging ability enabled me to escape the excruciating impact of this mistake. They said afterwards they'd only given me a child's whipping but I still bear the scars, physical as well as mental. The ship's surgeon ordered that I be birched. I was stretched across a bench with my arms and legs tied with canvas strips so I could not move. My trousers were pulled down. Then they birched me on my bare buttocks, swishing me with all the vigour they could in turn muster. I admit to you, Oliver, that I had hoped not to squeal but the pain was like nothing I had ever experienced. Soon I was screaming and sobbing uncontrollably. Only when they tired of their sport did they release me cut and bleeding, squirming with pain and humiliation. My buttocks felt like a white-hot ball of fire.

'So you see the voyage gave me plenty of time to reflect on my life and where it was leading. I didn't wish to receive further punishment and I recognized that the gallows would not be an attractive end. Fagin had taught me that and I love life too much to squander it on a hangman's noose. On our arrival, to my dismay I found the New World was little different from the old. Prostitution, robbery, blackmail, and murder are just as prevalent there as here. But I resisted the temptation to continue in my old ways. I was helped in my resolution by the fact that Australia does not have the same class-ridden prejudices of this damned society. There a man may be judged by his worth and not his birth, by his future rather than by his past. And I desperately wanted to put my past behind me. For several years I worked hard to show I was capable of being a new man. And I did convince those who mattered, though it was not easy. I avoided returning to drink and theft and I learnt the value of solid and honest hard work.

'With my credentials established, Oliver, I was able to attract the attention of a rich trader. I had the commitment and energy that he increasingly lacked, and so step by step he entrusted me with more and more of his business until eventually he made me his partner. My efforts transformed his business and my share of the profits enabled me to set myself up as an independent man. I've got a large farm to my name now and I am respected. It's ironic that, returning here, I remain just a convict.' The Dodger sensed my impatience. 'But enough of my history,' he said, 'Tell me what you want.'

I told my entire story as quickly as I could and he proved just as attentive a listener to me as I had been when he had narrated the story of his life. He heard all I had to say intently, only occasionally interrupting me to seek clarification on a point. To my surprise I could tell that he already knew much of what I told him. His manner towards me seemed to undergo a total transformation. When I had finished, he grasped me by my hand and shook it vigorously.

'I have to admire you, Oliver. Not many would have discovered so much — or wished to! You have convinced me that your motives are honourable and I will therefore take you to the only person who can answer all your remaining questions, providing you agree to being blindfolded.'

Needless to say, I nodded my assent. Dawkins led me back up the stairs and along the bridge to where a hackney carriage was waiting. Once I was aboard it, I submitted to the blindfold he had requested and we embarked on our mystery journey. I passed through the darkened city streets in a deeper darkness both of body and mind, wondering to whom I was being taken. The Dodger refused to speak further and we sat in an uneasy silence, broken only by the sound of the wheels of the hackney carriage and the horse's hoofs on the cobbles. After what seemed an eternity but in fact was probably no more than an hour or so, the carriage came to a halt and, still blindfolded, I disembarked into a darkened street. Dawkins spun me round so that I lost all sense of direction. Then he grasped my hand and led me through a couple of streets. We stopped and I heard him unlock a door. He guided me inside and led me up a flight of stairs. Again, I heard the unlocking of a door and we entered a room. I was pushed gently but firmly into a chair. He told me to stay quietly there until he could prepare the person he wanted me to see. Although I could easily have removed the blindfold, for my hands were untied, I refrained from doing so. And I waited in the darkness, the only sound that of a nearby ticking clock.

When Dawkins returned I could hear that he was helping someone into the room. I sensed that the person was moving slowly towards me and my whole body tensed. The person's hands touched my face and gently caressed it. The hands were soft and those of a woman. With an audible sob, the woman began untying my blindfold but the task seemed almost beyond her because her hands trembled so. I stayed rigid as if frozen to the spot. At last the blindfold fell away. There was nothing to be seen but only because, in my emotion, I had closed both eyes tightly shut. I opened my eyes and fainted with the shock of what I saw. It was Nancy.

18

The Murder of Nancy

When I opened my eyes she was still there. My sight had not deceived me. She looked much older than I would have expected and there was an extreme frailty about her that obviously caused the Dodger deep concern. But it was she. It was indeed Nancy and her eyes looked into mine with the same intense passion I had sensed all those years before.

Nancy broke the silence first. 'You've no idea, Oliver,' she said, 'how much I have both longed and dreaded our meeting again. There has never been a day since we last met that I have not thought of you and begged God's blessing on my poor boy. And now I see you I know you're such a fine young gentleman, so all my prayers have been answered. I am glad from what Jack tells me that you know as much as you do, although it was I who wanted so much to protect you from that knowledge.'

'But you were found dead,' I gasped. 'Your skull was shattered. Your features were bludgeoned into a pulp. Your blood was

273

splattered all over the room. The ashes of the club used to kill you were found in the grate, along with fragments of bloodstained cloth. The very feet of Sikes's dog were bloody. Bill died seeking your murderer. I attended your funeral.'

'It was not me who died in that room that night, Oliver. It was another. After Bill had left, I lay on the bed in a kind of semi-swoon. There was indeed a terrible gash on my forehead where in his fury he had struck me and, despite his attempts to stem the flow of blood, it was still bleeding profusely. Fleshy wounds of that sort often do. I am not sure how long I lay there. Bull's-eye for a time kept me company but I eventually tired of his piteous whining and, staggering to my feet, I threw him out. Yes, I believe his paws were covered with my blood. However, by then my head wound had ceased bleeding and I ripped up some pieces of cloth to mop up some of the blood that stained the floor. It was while I was engaged in that task that I heard the stealthy approach of someone up the stairs. Fearing it might be someone sent by Fagin, I seized the only thing in the room available to protect myself: the club that Bill had used to hit me and which, in detestation of his actions, he had left behind.

'The door was unlocked and I had not time

to find the key, which had been displaced in my fight with Bill. I therefore took refuge behind the table and, with beating heart, awaited my visitor. When the door opened I breathed a sigh of relief and dropped the club because it was only Charlotte Bolter, or rather, to give her the name I now know to be her true one, Charlotte Sowerberry. I had had little to do with her because she had only recently joined our group, having come to London with her lover, Morris Bolter, or should I say, Noah Claypole. The little I had seen had not impressed me. She seemed to lack everything. Her looks were poor, her dress slovenly, her brain slow, and her tongue quick but stupid. The best Fagin could do with her was to assign her to steal from little children. As far as I knew her one saving grace was her obvious obsession with her lover, but even that lacked attraction because her choice of man was a pretty poor specimen.'

The Dodger could not help laughing at this. 'You're a fine one to talk, Nancy. Most of us could nivver see what you saw in Bill, brute that he was.'

'I won't deny Bill had his faults, especially when he had been drinking, but he didn't deceive and use me the way Noah Claypole did Charlotte. She was expected to wait on him hand and foot. Not that she was meek and mild by temperament. Far from it. Oliver had told me enough of her treatment of him to make me realize what a cow she really was. And on this occasion I saw the worst of her. She had discovered from one of the lads that Fagin had sent Noah to my place. Everyone knew Fagin was desperate to drive a wedge between me and Bill and, foolishly, she believed that Noah had been selected to win over my affections. As if he could! Only Charlotte could believe Noah to be so special. Sick though I still felt, I could not hide my amusement when she challenged me with seeking to seduce her man.

'My cruel laughter was a mistake, but I made matters worse by comparing Claypole to Bill and telling her exactly what Bill would do to her precious Noah if he ever approached me. My words seemed to make her view the gash on my forehead and the bloody marks around the room in a new and horrible light. She became irrational, convinced that Bill had found Noah and me together and had punished both him and me. She could see what he had done to me, but what had he done to Noah? And where were they now? With mounting panic that paid no heed to what I was trying to say to her, she looked around her. Then she saw Bill's bloody club and the bloody pawmarks of his dog. Screaming obscenities at me, she launched herself across the room towards me.

'Weakened by loss of blood, I knew I would be no match for her. I pushed the table at her to give me a momentary advantage and, picking up the club, swung it at her as hard as I could. She fell backwards on the grate and her head struck the iron fender. She lay still. I thought myself fortunate to have knocked her out with just the one blow, but then I noticed the blood trickling from the back of her neck. Kneeling down, I lifted her head and realized that her skull was cracked and she was dead. The poor unfortunate woman must have had some weakness there for her to die so easily. Looking at her corpse, I confess I panicked. Already people called me a whore and a thief, now they would call me a murderess. No one would believe it to be an accident. The pictures of the gallows that Fagin showed me as a child came flashing into my mind. I felt as if I was as good as dead.

'And then I had an idea. Charlotte and I were about the same size. What if people thought the dead body was mine? The finger of suspicion would fall on Fagin. Everyone in the gang knew he was out to get me. In my confused state, I didn't imagine they would think it was Bill. Although he was rough at times, I thought everyone knew he loved me too much to be my murderer. With the police after Fagin, he would have to take flight and his gang would break up. They would no longer be a threat to my son or to me, and I could seek a new life. Mr Brownlow and Rose Maylie had promised me they would do all in their power to give me a new start in a new country if I wished it. With the threat of Fagin removed, I was sure you, Oliver, would be recognized as the half-brother of Edward Leeford and become a wealthy man. And that was all I wanted for you. I did not wish you to know who your real mother was. It was better I lived so far away that I would never be tempted to try and see you. The one problem I could foresee was persuading Bill to come with me, but I was confident I could achieve that.

'And so I stripped Charlotte of her clothes, took off my garments, and put them on to her. Then came the worst part. I covered the body with a rug so that I did not have to see exactly what I was doing and I battered her head repeatedly with the club so that her face would be unrecognizable. I then threw the instrument into the fire lest it provide any clues as to its user. And thus I murdered myself.'

She paused and looked to see my reaction,

dreading lest I reject her. But how could I? She was my mother. My loving mother, more sinned against than sinning, who had risked everything for me. I clutched her frail body to me and repeatedly but gently kissed her careworn face. Our joint tears gave expression to my forgiveness and her contrition. I could sense that even the hardened Dodger was moved by the signs of our mutual love. And when the intensity of our embrace had ended, my mother slowly gathered herself together and resumed her story:

'I fled from the room, disguised in Charlotte's clothes. My intention was to hide and get a message to Bill about my whereabouts. But that is when everything went wrong. As I crossed through an alleyway, a richly clothed child recognized Charlotte's dress and called out that I was the lady who had robbed him the previous day. His father shouted out *thief!* and promised a guinea to any man who would seize hold of me till the police could be brought. Before I knew where I was, I was being pursued. Weakened from loss of blood and from all my exertions, I slipped and fell very heavily down a flight of stairs, knocking myself uncon-scious.

'When I eventually came round I found myself in a hospital bed. When my body had been turned over in the street, the child had confessed I was a different lady from the one who had stolen from him. His father, mortified at causing an innocent woman such an injury, had paid for me to be looked after. The nurse told me I was lucky to be alive and that I had been in a coma for over a fortnight.

'I released myself from the hospital as soon as I could. By then, of course, it was too late. You can imagine my horror when I discovered that Bill had been accused of my murder and had been killed trying to escape. My one consolation was that the rest of my plan had worked better than I had envisaged and that Fagin was on trial and his hanging a foregone conclusion. Your own future, Oliver, was secured. I rapidly came to the conclusion that it was better if you and the whole world thought me dead, and so I sought out Mr Brownlow. Swearing him to secrecy, I told him what I have told you about Charlotte's death. He was true to his earlier promise and gave me recommendations to start a new life abroad. I suspect he was rather glad to free himself and you of my presence.

'My life since then, Oliver, has been a good one. No son would find fault with the tenor of my life over these past few years. I made the most of my new start and a couple of years ago had the good fortune to meet the

Dodger, who had also done very well for himself. He has risked everything to bring me back to England. I had no intention of finding you again, but I hoped to be able to see you without your being aware of my presence. I wanted to see what had happened to my son before I died.'

'Died?'

'Look at her, Oliver,' interrupted the Dodger. 'You can see she is very sick, very sick indeed. If the truth be told it is only her determination to see you that has kept her alive. Though she is ashamed to tell you herself, her physical and, increasingly, her mental frailty are due to the fact she is entering the last stages of syphilis. We've both seen enough of the rashes produced by the disease to recognize its symptoms all too well. She has been taking some arsenic to try and keep it at bay.'

Nancy looked at me and whispered, 'Sadly I have found you cannot escape your past.'

'So have I,' I replied and clutched her thin frame to my chest. My heart felt as if it would break.

And so I was reunited with my mother, but not for long. On closer acquaintance it became all too obvious that the terrible disease she had contracted had already affected her in a variety of ways, weakening her constitution, limiting her movements, impairing her concentration and affecting her judgement. Her body was covered with itchy rashes and sores that gave her leopard-like blotches on her skin. She also had an agonizing pain in her back and there was a kind of inflammation in her joints that made them stiff and swollen so that any movement was painful. It was not uncommon for her to burn up with fever and increasingly she could not find rest in sleep. Her determination to see me had held the disease at bay, but, now that we were together, her physical state rapidly declined. Her speech became ever more slurred and at times we could not understand what she was trying to say. Some days she would appear almost paralysed but then violent convulsions would occur and she would suddenly roar and rage like an animal in a cage, lashing out at anyone near her in her agony.

However, far worse than the relentless physical deterioration was the increasing mental effect of the disease. Sometimes she had bouts when she lost all touch with reality and suffered from strange delusions, while at other times she appeared disorientated or strangely and sadly apathetic. There were days when she was so racked by hallucinations that we had no option but to physically restrain her. Worst of all, her memory became obviously faulty so that on occasion she could not recall words or phrases and this added to the physical difficulties she was having in making herself understood. There were even times when she could not remember who she was or where she was and then she could not recognize either the Dodger or me. Those days were the worst.

And yet very occasionally Nancy still had better days in which she appeared more like herself. At such times she told me she was now content to die, knowing that I was well situated. It was her way of reinforcing to me, that having been reunited with her son, she no longer cared about resisting the effects of the appalling disease. The Dodger and I agreed to tell Dickens what had happened because we both recognized that it was safer to ensure that his investigative powers were taken off the case. However, we swore him to secrecy and I informed Rose and Harry that my search had come to a dead end. Although I hated to deceive them, I knew that the fewer who knew of Nancy's existence the more likelihood there was that I could keep her secret safe from the authorities. Desperately ill though Nancy was, we feared she would face the gallows if her murder of Charlotte became a matter for police investigation.

Dickens came only once to the house where we tended her, and neither the Dodger nor I was allowed to be present for their meeting. Fortunately his arrival coincided with one of her better days. I cannot tell you what was said for both found it too painful to speak of what they shared, but I sensed that both forgave each other for past wrongs. Dickens was certainly deeply moved. Both he and I encouraged the Dodger, good friend though he had proved to be to Nancy, to return to his new life abroad before the authorities caught up with him. With sadness, he agreed because he knew he could do no more for her. However, their parting, which took place in one of Nancy's few more rational phases, was a painful one. They had shared much together and the Dodger's loyalty and love had been significant in helping her face her declining health. I too was sorry to see him leave because his care for my mother had made me long since forgive his role in leading me as a child into Fagin's clutches.

Nancy's parting from the Dodger was perhaps her last truly distressing moment, but it was not mine. Nancy had no wish to let the disease totally destroy her brain and on those days when she had moments of lucidity she begged me to end her life before her mind was lost for ever.

'Oliver, my brain is on fire. It feels as if my entire body is being simultaneously bitten by adders and hacked to pieces by knives. No torture rack could match what I feel and I am slowly but surely having all my memories scattered away like dust. You know there are days when I cannot even remember words let alone recognize you. This is no life for me and I hate you having to see me like this. Please, I beg you, I implore you, if you love me take steps to end my existence before madness takes me over completely. I've seen enough of what the final stages of this disease can do to fear what will happen next. One woman whom I knew ended her days howling like an animal while another began collecting and drinking her urine because in her mind it had become the elixir of life. Is that the kind of existence you want me to endure? Do you want to see me a chained and bound madwoman, my brain eaten away?'

At first I refused to contemplate what she desired but, after one especially bad day when I feared there was only a very short time before I was doomed to tend only her physical shell, I became more receptive to her pleas. I was constantly praying to God that she should be allowed to retain some shreds of reason and recognition in her syphilitic frame, but in my heart I increasingly feared that she was right and that I would be reduced to tending a raving madwoman. Death appeared a welcome alternative to a life in which the real Nancy no longer existed. And Nancy, even in the final stages of her illness, proved stronger than I. One evening her feeble hand grasped mine and, looking at me through dilated eyes with such deep love that I wept, she struggled to speak in a voice I could understand. At last by an intense act of will she mastered control of her quivering mouth and whispered:

'Don't let me die a stranger to you, Oliver. You have borne much in your life and I do not want you to bear that.'

'I can bear anything but losing you,' I sobbed.

'But lose me you must, Oliver and, much though I love you, I want to die with dignity. My life has contained precious little of that. Please, I beg you not to let me continue with this slow creeping death which unrelentingly eats away at both my mind and body.'

Her life had indeed had little dignity and was I to deny her one remaining wish? I knew in my heart of hearts that Nancy, whatever the sins of her youth, did not deserve a living death. And so the two of us said our final farewells — I cannot bring myself to write how painful that was to me — and then I placed a pillow over those features I had come to love so much. And, God forgive me, I murdered Nancy.

We do hope that you have enjoyed reading this large print book.

Did you know that all of our titles are available for purchase?

We publish a wide range of high quality large print books including:
Romances, Mysteries, Classics
General Fiction
Non Fiction and Westerns

Special interest titles available in large print are:
The Little Oxford Dictionary
Music Book
Song Book
Hymn Book
Service Book

Also available from us courtesy of Oxford University Press:
Young Readers' Dictionary
(large print edition)
Young Readers' Thesaurus
(large print edition)

For further information or a free brochure, please contact us at:
Ulverscroft Large Print Books Ltd.,
The Green, Bradgate Road, Anstey,
Leicester, LE7 7FU, England.
Tel: (00 44) **0116 236 4325**
Fax: (00 44) **0116 234 0205**

Other titles published by
The House of Ulverscroft:

MURDER IN MIND

J. A. O'Brien

As acting DI, Andy Lukeson had not expected to head up a high-profile murder investigation, but there he is, thrust forward into the limelight, investigating the murder of a woman whose death may be linked to a string of murders long unsolved. As he struggles to find the killer, Lukeson's fears of the case going cold haunt his every waking moment. Can he get to the heart of the matter before it's too late?

STONE COLD

Peter Taylor

Former gypsy prize-fighter, Henry Torrance, is about to be released from prison where he's been serving time for killing fellow bare-knuckle fighter Bull Jackson. Now, he's resolved to get his life on track and settle down with his girlfriend Mary. However, the criminal Jackson family is insistent that Henry should fight their latest protege and Henry's brother and father accept the challenge on his behalf. As the day of the big fight draws closer, Henry's determination not to return to his old ways is countered by the mounting pressure on him. Can he ever escape his dark past?

LOVE TO DEATH

Patti Battison

What happens when love goes bad — and it becomes an obsession . . . ? Ageing rocker Johnny Lee Rogers is performing a series of charity concerts in Larchborough. His biggest fan, librarian Lizzie Thornton, has won tickets to see his final show. She's convinced that Fate is bringing them together . . . and Lizzie's always wanted a December wedding. As the town basks in the hottest temperatures for decades, it will be no Summer of Love for DCI Paul Wells and his team. Lizzie, a group of travellers and a missing girl seem to have conspired to bring a time of torment, intrigue and murder.

WEB OF DECEIT

Peter Conway

When prominent neurosurgeon Richard Kershaw is found dead in his house on a Sunday afternoon, his friends and family are shocked. Handsome and charismatic, the husband of an aristocratic and the father of adorable children, Kershaw always seemed happy and successful in so many ways. Before his killer is discovered, however, a darker side to Kershaw's character is revealed. As his secrets unravel, the lives of those who knew him will be changed forever . . .

FLOTSAM & JETSAM

Keith Moray

The Flotsam & Jetsam TV show gained a cult following throughout Scotland by highlighting that money could be made from the debris that washed up onto remote beaches. When it came to West Uist, it brought the exciting prospect of celebrity status for the locals. Then, one fateful night, everything changed . . . The death of a noted scientist, the discovery of a half-drowned puppy and the suggestion of police negligence now lead Inspector Torquil McKinnon to investigate sinister events on the seemingly idyllic island. Who knows what other secrets will be washed ashore?

VILLAGE FATE

Jean Saunders

In Somerset, in Bately-sub-Mendip, Pargeter's doll factory burns down and a man's body is discovered inside. When the missing, elderly factory owner, Edith Pargeter is found drowned in a ditch, village librarian Rosie Redman suspects that Edith's brother, Edgar, was responsible for both Edith's death and that of her sister Edna six months earlier. So Rosie enlists the help of the local reporter, Charlie Walters, to investigate privately. However, her involvement antagonises the police who want them to stop interfering. But would-be-sleuth Rosie continues to throw suspicion on Edgar — despite Charlie's warning that she could be playing a very dangerous game . . .